also available by Nirmal Verma
from Readers International:

The World Elsewhere

The Crow
Deliverar

The Crows of Deliverance

stories by Nirmal Verma

translated from Hindi by Kuldip Singh
and Jai Ratan

readers international

The stories in this book were first published in Hindi and appeared in various collections. The essay "The Short Story as a Pure Literary Form" first appeared in *Word and Memory*, published in 1988 by Vagdevi Prakashan Publishers, India.

First published in English by Readers International Inc., and Readers International, London. Editorial inquiries to London office at 8 Strathray Gardens, London NW3 4NY, England. US/Canadian inquiries to Subscriber Service Department, P.O.Box 959, Columbia LA 71418-0959 USA.

This translation was made possible in part through a grant from the Arts Council of Great Britain.

 The story "Amalya" is translated by Jai Ratan. All other stories in this volume are translated by Kuldip Singh.

Cover art: *Widows of Urindaban* (1987), painting by Indian artist Arpana Caur, courtesy of The October Gallery, London
Cover design by Jan Brychta
Printed in Malta by Interprint Limited

Library of Congress Catalog Card Number: 91-60878

British Library Cataloging in Publication Data
Verma, Nirmal 1929-
The Crows of Deliverance.
1. Hindi fiction. Short stories
I. Title
891.4337 [F]

ISBN 0-930523-79-2 Hardcover
ISBN 0-930523-80-6 Paperback

Contents

Contents

Introduction:
The Short Story as a Pure Literary Form

In recent decades, forms of literary expression seem to have shed much of their exclusive, closely-guarded autonomy. They freely mingle with one another, journalism with literature, fiction with reportage; and such acts of promiscuous union, if and when successfully realised – for example, in Nabokov's *Pale Fire* or Mailer's *Armies of the Night* – evoke in us a complex response which cannot easily be defined in terms of conventional literary categories. That a specific literary genre may have some inviolable purity seems to have too much of the hot house about it, in which a Mallarmé could happily bloom, but a Mailer would surely feel suffocated. We have drifted, so far as prose is concerned, into an era of open-air and open-ended literary forms.

Nevertheless, even if the boundaries are blurred, the distinctions between a story, a poem, a novel still persist. Structures have surely loosened, but they have not disintegrated. A story doesn't become less of a story if it abandons its familiar mode of narration: a poetic metaphor may transfix a landscape and an obsessive image may illuminate an incident far more effectively than the simple narration of what happened next; but the metaphor in the story still seeks a "body" to make the meaningful gesture – the body of prose. And the reverse can also happen: a poem may unfold itself in a story – Pushkin's *Eugene Onegin* is an example – but the incidents of the story acquire relevance only in the "space" given to them by the poem; for it is the poem that conveys the ultimate experience.

Thus the choice of forms cannot be arbitrary; it is inherent in the nature of experience itself. We cannot transfer the same experience from one form to another without deadening its quick throb. Once dead, it can be transferred anywhere, to a play or a poem or a story; but it would be a dead play, a dead poem and a sad story. It is not that a writer first has a certain experience and then he embodies it in a particular art form, rather it is the experience which chooses its own form to make its presence felt. Thus we cannot say that a particular experience has been "captured" in a story; there is no capturing in the realm of art. What is more correct is that a certain experience could realise itself only in the form of a story, and in no other form.

We read stories in words, but are these the same words we read in a poem or a newspaper report? In the latter they lead somewhere, are used as a means. They offer information about the world and its people. Once consumed, the words exhaust their meaning. In a poem words enjoy a greater degree of sovereignty. They act as self-contained units of meaning, refusing to serve an end outside themselves. But in a story the words acquire a luminous tension because they are neither fully sovereign in their own right nor totally subservient to an external end: a short story is a "report" on the outside world transformed into the language of its own truth. Hovering between life and art, the truth of the story is embedded in words which string themselves into sentences, one leading to another, weaving a web in which the quick of life is caught. But the writer is no spider catching a fly coming from outside. It is in the very process of spinning sentences that the truth of the story unfolds itself, and the life which is caught in the web is indistinguishable from the threads of which it is woven. In the art of short story the web and the fly are always the same.

Thus what we regard as the "purity" of art form is nothing but the total identification of form and vision. The content of the story can be paraphrased or expanded in several ways, but the form in which the vision is embodied remains unique and inviolable. The innate and ultimate experience of a Chekhov story lies not in what the story "says", for what he said had often been told already by several of his contemporaries. What makes his stories so distinct and memorable is that chaste intensity which enables us to touch the very flesh of life when we are really touching the body of his prose. Here the words are used neither as self-contained units nor merely as a means to convey information; they only create an amplitude where everything *is*, and nothing is explained.

But this concept of purity in narrative prose could only appear at a time when the short story had already acquired a life of its own. For it to develop in its modern form, the short story had to wait for the advent of the printing press so that it could be presented to the public in its own right. Not that stories were not written earlier, but they were more in the nature of fables (*Panchtantra*) or romances like *The Arabian Nights* or Boccaccio's *Decameron*. By and large, they were part of an oral tradition, where the stories were still told to the members of a community who had certain common points of reference and shared the same memories. The author or narrator often remained anonymous, for he was as much a part of the audience as the stories he shared with them.

But the short story as we know it differed from them not merely because it was printed, but in a more fundamental sense in that it was the product of an imagination which was essentially private, rooted in the individual consciousness of the author whose signature was imprinted on it. And paradoxical as it may seem, it was precisely in this phase of its development that the short story extricated itself from its regional eccentricities and acquired a cosmopolitan character. It was no mere accident that a Parisian poet like Baudelaire could so intensely respond to the peculiarly obsessive tales of an American writer, Edgar Allan Poe. Even the writers of the so-called Third World could not keep themselves immune from its ubiquitous impact. As late as the second decade of the twentieth century, Hindi writer Prem Chand was hungrily devouring much of the fiction being published in Europe, but especially nineteenth-century Russian short stories.

Both for its autonomy and universality, the short story was indeed indebted to the novel, which in the earlier phase of its development cleared the ground for the emergence of narrative as an independent form, secular in tone and content, completely free from theological and mythological wrappings. Furthermore, the novel, as it reached maturity, asserted its independence from the all-prevailing canons of bourgeois morality. Indeed, the much abused dictum "art for Art's sake" in its time was not a flight from reality, but an affirmation of the supremacy of art against the banal and degraded versions of "reality". It may surprise many of us that the concept of purity in art, which in our so-called "revolutionary" age bears the stigma of ivory-tower elitism, in its origins was characterised by the most uncompromising act of courage on the part of artists to live as exiles in a society in which they no longer believed. To affirm the purity and autonomy of art implied the rejection of the false consciousness of the society they lived in. It was the moment when the act of aesthetic freedom became the symbol of moral protest. It would also explain the agony of a Flaubert who went on writing his novels while never ceasing to despise his public.

It is strange that it was during the depressing decades of the late nineteenth century that the short story found its inner, authentic voice. As one reads the stories of Tolstoy, Chekhov and Maupassant, one is amazed how so fragile a form – in their hands – can bear the burden of intense personal anguish and at the same time be an austere but lucid comment on the oppressive social conditions prevailing at that time. Hereafter the short story ceased to be the poor relation of the novel and came to acquire an aura of its own. The emotional co-ordinates it determined for itself retained much of the lyricism of the old tales, but the area of experience it chose for itself was very different from that of the novel.

Did the difference between the two literary forms lie merely in the shortness of the narrative? Because of its brevity, was it less expressive, less inclusive in its comprehension of the human situation? V.S.Pritchett, in explaining the distinction, has said, "The novel tends to tell us everything, whereas the short story tends to tell one thing – and that intensely". Is it really so? What exactly do we mean by "one thing", and does "everything" in the novel really encompass everything that a person undergoes from the time of his birth till the moment he dies? All such quantitative criteria prove inadequate to define the distinction when applied to really significant works of art. Tolstoy's story *The Death of Ivan Ilich* indeed deals with one thing, the act of dying, but does it not include "everything", at least everything that matters, that Ivan Ilich has gone through in his entire life? The story precisely concentrates on one crucial moment which in its unredeemed despair and darkness illuminates all the preceding moments of his life – thereby demolishing all the academic distinctions between "one" and "many". And what about *Mrs Dalloway*? In this full-length novel the writer seems to be concerned, not with the entire life of her heroine, but only with very selective moments, with what Virginia Woolf would call "moments of vision", while the rest of Mrs Dalloway's life remains a closed book, safely locked in the past, to which we have no access. And so one wonders if the Upanishadic wisdom implied in seeing "one in many and many in one" should guide us in not making too neat a distinction between the different literary genres.

And yet the short story differs significantly from the novel, though not in the manner in which Mr Pritchett would like to make it. The distinction lies not between one and many, not in the length and number of details, but in the author's *attitude* to them, to the form in which they begin to breathe a life of their own. The vision implied in a short story need not be less complete and comprehensive than that of a novel, but within that vision every detail of the story acquires a different tone and tension. Instead of using details as a means to produce a cumulative effect at the end, each detail serves as a nerve centre pulsating with a life of its own, and when the end comes, nothing is concluded, for nothing has really begun. Of course, on the surface of the printed page the story does begin at one point and ends at another, but on the surface of consciousness, only a tip of life is visible, aglow with its own light. The short story does not flow within the river of time, as the novel does, but remains congealed in a pool which is static; a static time of memory, where the only motion is that of remembrance. The novel uses memory as a "struggle against the power of time"; but in a story there still persists that archaic element where things are remembered not against time but in the backdrop of time, as it were. And that is why a story leans more heavily on language than a novel: words correspond with the events one tries to recall, rather than being used as a means to evoke the memory of that which is past.

And this brings me to another crucial difference. It is a peculiar thing about the individual consciousness that, when reflected in a certain time-scale, it inevitably assumes the narrative form of the novel; and when it is condensed in the timeless anatomy of words, it grows into a poem. But what happens to it when it tries to defy the continuity of time, yet resists being subsumed within the autonomous configuration of words? At such a moment, a literary form is created – half way between a novel and a poem – which we may call by the name of story; but it is essentially rooted in the deep longing to stretch the time of a poem within the narrative space which belongs to the novel. Shall we then say that what the short story attempts to do is to cover a no-man's land between language and time – poem and history – in its brief span of life?

To be poetic in structure and yet be narrative in intent, that seems to be the feat akin to tight-rope walking that is called for. And it is precisely this which comes to mind in the remarkable purity of detail and ascetic brilliance in stories by Isaak Babel and Hemingway, Katherine Mansfield and D.H. Lawrence. Nearer home, Manik Bandopadhyay and Prem Chand display the same power in their short stories, perhaps more than in their novels. All these writers, so different from one another, have something in common. It is what Thomas Mann once described as the combination of "precision with passion". It was Babel who in his stories made that incisive thrust into the history of his time, not by delineation of facts and events, but by means of a bare and sharp image of the neck of a goose being squeezed and the blood gushing out – and that single image conveys in a few words all the horror and the dark passions of the war, which no war novel could ever describe. And was it not Chekhov who once advised Gorki that the reflection of the moon in a broken piece of bottle is all you need to describe the city moonlight? If Babel metamorphoses history into a poetic image, then Chekhov at the opposite end transfixes a poetic image in the calm flow of his narrative prose. And to be able to do so without resorting to the lyricism of the poem or to the narrative time of the novel is precisely the challenge which the short story accepts in order to evoke that particular response in us which purely belongs to its province.

The same challenge was posed to the Hindi short story, but in an entirely different context and with a different set of tensions. In a traditional society like India literature becomes, more often than not, an appendage to religion or social ideologies without having an independent identity of its own. It is too large a question to discuss here whether the separation of art as an atomised activity has not led to the impoverishment and devaluation of literature in the West. On the other hand, if literature remains too long submerged in the motley concerns of society, the danger is that it becomes a mere parasite on theology or politics, rather than having an innate quality of its own voice. Thus in the beginning of the twentieth century, the Hindi short story had to emancipate itself from various socio-religious encumbrances to develop itself into an independent literary genre. This could not have been achieved without undergoing a long, torturous process of secularization, in the widest sense of the word. If with Prem Chand, the Hindi short story matured into an art form, it was also because he was the most secular writer of his time.

But "secularism" in art is not an unmixed blessing. In a society like ours it reflects the slow process of disintegration of what earlier constituted the "religious habitat" of its people. Exiled from the "home" which was once provided by myths and symbols, the Indian middle class was thrown into the arid openness of a secular age. Emancipation from the past inevitably led to a state of alienation in the present – and it was the short story which reflected most powerfully this state of spiritual desolation. While the Indian novel, with few exceptions, still clung to the lost purity of moral ideals (Tagore's *Gora* is a case in point), the short story did not shirk from fathoming the morass of impurities which engulfed Indian life.

And this is the paradox of narrative art: what we regard as the "purity" of form is actually built up through the multiple impurities of experience which life presents to us. We love and we hate and we suffer, and all the time we are engulfed by a maze of experiences which seem to have no pattern, no rational order. The more helpless and bewildered we find ourselves, the greater is the temptation to fall victim to cults, or ideologies which claim to rationalise everything in terms of psychological and historical explanations. As the crisis deepens, shriller and louder become the voices of prophets among the ruins. And art itself seems to be overwhelmed by these voices. Where it refuses to speak the language of the preachers, it may well be forced to remain silent. And to silence it has been reduced in those parts of the world where language at its very source has been corrupted. Again it was Isaak Babel, one of the most remarkable story writers of modern times, who in a speech to the Soviet Writers' Conference said, "I am practising a new literary genre, the genre of silence." But then silence itself can be dangerous to those who live on slogans; Babel perished in a labour camp.

But it does teach us a lesson. In the modern world, where all manner of tricks and terrors are exercised to compromise the human conscience, art in its freedom is perhaps most deeply committed to the language of truth, without which all social commitments lose their value. You corrupt the language before you destroy the man; or perhaps you don't have to destroy, he exists no more once his language is dead. Thus when we speak of the short story as a pure literary form, we are not speaking of any esoteric mystique of Art, but actually dealing with the imaginative power of language, uninterrupted by external voices, so that we can hear the whisper of truth in its own words. Artistic forms may be universal, but artistic truths are not. They are invariably embodied in the language in which they are communicated. And this language is to be defended if art and human dignity are to survive in our time.

The Crows of Deliverance

The Crows of Deliverance

Amalya

Gently placing my hand on his shoulder, I led him up the stairs from the basement. He was still shivering with cold and passed his trembling hand over his face, as if wiping the vestiges of sleep from his forehead down to his chin.

"Son of a bitch!" he said.

"Not so loud. He may be listening." I dragged him to the outside door. Both of us lingered at the threshold for a while. Who would care to stir out in such piercing cold?

We heard the girl's laughter behind the door – strong, soft and clear.

I pushed the door open. Outside the darkness of a November night covered all. Under the pale lamp-light our shadows wavered like thieves.

"Shameless! Stupid!" he cried.

I did not stop him from speaking. Now there was no one around to hear.

We stopped after walking some distance. Turning back, we gazed at the building which housed our basement – below the road, hidden in the dark, with its rows of beds like a hospital ward.

After wandering aimlessly in the city all day, we would return to the basement in the evening, where an acrid smell would greet us. Whether it was the smell of stale air or of our unwashed, damp beds, it was difficult to say. We had long since given up hazarding a guess about it. We feared that it could also be the smell of dead rats, though we never said so.

Every morning we would go to the Ministry's office and wait. They had told us that as soon as our papers were ready, we would be sent to another city. But we were never told which city. We were not worried though. We knew it would be like any other city, just as new and strange as this one.

We would wait in that office for long hours. In those days the waiting did not jar on us, as we had a lot of time on our hands. Besides, while cooling our heels there we were spared the foul smell of the basement and its chill humidity. After all, it was preferable to wait within the four walls of a familiar office than slog around unfamiliar city streets.

"Don't you like it here?" A middle-aged woman who worked in the office would put this question to us almost every day. She was a sympathetic, kindly woman who felt bad when she saw us wasting our time there. She thought we could spend it in more pleasant and worthwhile ways. In the beginning, she had even given us passes for an evening at the opera, compliments of the Ministry. She thought this way we would not feel lonely in the evenings. But when she found that we just tucked the passes in our pockets without making use of them, she felt greatly disappointed.

"It's only a matter of a few days more," she would say, giving us a despairing look. We knew this was a hint for us to leave. We would thank her, take her formal handshake and depart.

We never cared to find out who among us went

where during the course of the day. But the one who arrived back first in the evening would invariably wait for the others. Only the Brazilian rarely went out, staying in the basement most of the time. When I returned in the evening I would find him lying in his bed. His guitar would be at rest in the chair and his mother's photograph, as usual, planted at the table. He had shown me the photograph on the very first day. It had put me in a quandary. If it were a wife's or sweetheart's photo, one could without hesitation say that she looked so charming or beautiful. But what kind of comment could one make about a mother, even if she was beautiful, as was the case with the Brazilian's? Had he not told me it was his mother, I might unwittingly have said too much. Anticipating some such thing, he had perhaps thought it discreet to inform me at the start.

"How is the weather outside?" he would ask, still lying in his bed.

"Like yesterday," I would reply.

"Today it was very chilly here," he would tell me.

"We had a short spell of sunshine, though the cold was as severe as yesterday."

We would talk in this way, reeling out one sentence after another as in those phrase-books for foreign tourists. We also conveyed our meanings by gestures. But we would soon get bored. We had not developed that sense of intimacy which alone could fill the vacuum between language and gesture. It needed patience and familiarity to cultivate that intimacy. And we were too submerged in the day's routine to make the effort.

Sometimes it also happens that two people cannot talk with complete openness unless a third is present.

So it was with us. If the Arab hadn't come, we would have stayed tongue-tied in our beds.

The Arab would generally arrive late, and that lent him even more distinction. We were curious to know what he did in the unknown city until so late at night. No doubt he was conscious of his singularity in our eyes; he seemed quite vain about it. Coming into the basement, he would take off his overcoat with exaggerated care, after which he would remove his jacket, followed by his trousers and underwear, as if we were not there. This done, he would go and stand before the mirror, combing his curly hair. He would give us an unconcerned look, as if we did not exist, as if he were not sharing the same basement we were.

"Have you eaten?" he would ask.

"No." We could not admit to ourselves that we had been waiting for him.

He would open his suitcase to take out a change of clothes. It was a beautiful leather suitcase, yellow in colour. It must have been quite heavy even now. On the day of his arrival the Brazilian and I had had to help him lug it down the stairs. That night he had opened it before going to sleep, while we stood by as curious onlookers. First he had taken out two dinner suits and half a dozen nylon shirts, followed by ties of variegated patterns and colours, handkerchiefs and underwear. We watched, fascinated. Suddenly he stopped and looked at us. "Want to see something more?" He smiled like a conjurer before opening his Pandora's box.

He took out a couple of silk scarves, ladies' nylon stockings, bracelets and a string of pearls.

"Forty dollars," he said.

"Forty dollars?" the Brazilian's eyes opened wide

in surprise.

"You can't get these things over here," the Arab said.

"Are you going to sell them?"

"I have not come here to open a shop." The Arab gave us a contemptuous look. "How long have you been here?" His tone was tinged with derision.

"Today it is my fifth day," the Brazilian spread out his five fingers in the air. We had come at the same time, but I did not know he had been counting the days so assiduously.

The Arab nodded and proceeded to close his suitcase. We appeared to have fallen in his esteem.

The restaurant was not far from our basement. But we had to walk through dark lanes to reach it, and the distance seemed to be unending.

The streets were flanked by tall, decrepit buildings on both sides. Sometimes there was a gap with piles of rubble in front, reminding us of the destruction during the last war. On moonlit nights we would discover strange things in these pyramids of rubble – dolls, shaving brushes, newspapers fifteen or sixteen years old. The Brazilian would often rummage for such things and bring them back with him to the basement. The Arab and myself would find this habit of his laughable, even though we too kept our eyes alert to spot any worthwhile finds. It was an ancient city, and on moonlit nights we had an eerie feeling that there must be something mysterious embedded under each stone and every crumbling wall. We had only to extend our hands to take hold of the thing; it was just waiting to be picked up.

One night the Arab found something that quite astonished us – a violin, genuine and complete! It was lying in the ruins of a house. The Arab examined it, turning it from one side to the other. "Looks like it belonged to some Jew," he remarked at last.

"How do you know?" the Brazilian asked.

"Who else could it belong to?" the Arab said.

The Brazilian could not answer the Arab's seemingly irrefutable comment. But what the Arab did next roused our anger. He hid the violin in the same place where he had discovered it. "If you don't require it, give it to me," the Brazilian said. "I'll take it home."

"No, you're not taking it anywhere," the Arab said decisively.

I have little interest in music, but I too was not prepared to see the violin abandoned. Sensing our displeasure, the Arab said, "One should not pick up a dead man's things – even if he was a Jew."

"How do you know he's dead?" I asked him.

"Even if he's alive we should not touch his things," the Arab said. "He may turn up any moment to retrieve them."

We did not take kindly to his attitude. But when we looked at the crumbling and broken walls drenched in moonlight, we felt a sense of relief: the violin had gone back to where it belonged. Now nobody could take   it away.

We would stay in the restaurant till midnight. The Arab and I drank in moderation, but the Brazilian would not touch liquor. Once we had tried to force it on him. But after drinking half a glass of beer, he had vomited double the quantity on to the table. After that we did not insist further. When we drank too much and were merry, he would just sit there scowling, without wasting words on us, until we felt uncomfortable enough to leave.

Once outside, we would start talking volubly. We felt less lonely than we felt back in the basement. On our way back from the restaurant we would come across couples standing at their doors, whispering sweet nothings to each other. The Arab would whistle at them. They would turn back to look and laugh. Sometimes we almost brushed against them, but even that could not make them conscious of our presence.

"Don't they feel the cold?" the Brazilian would ask.

"Of course they feel the cold," the Arab would say. "That's why they're clinging to each other."

We could see the girls' white frocks etched against the night, and a smell would ooze from them which bore no relation to the past or the future. It was the kind of smell that floats in the air of ancient cities. It tingled our nerves.

Once in the basement, we would slip quietly into our beds. Except for the scurrying of rats, everything was silent. Only once I heard a soft murmur and sat up, shaken. The Brazilian had lit a candle in front of his mother's photograph. His eyes were closed, and his lips were moving. Perhaps he was praying before going to sleep. After a while the candle went out, but a gray murkiness crept about the basement.

Through our skylight appeared the feet of passers-by on the road above. Long legs and short legs, high heels and tiny, puppet-like feet, but nothing above the knees. One could not see their faces, but tried to imagine them from their feet. Till I fell asleep I could keep looking at the Theatre of the Road from my bed.

That night we had waited for the Arab to return. He habitually kept late hours, but never so late as this. As we left to eat, we had stuck a note on the basement door telling him we were at the restaurant. But it was still there when we returned.

"I don't know where he could have gone," the Brazilian said anxiously.

"He has many friends here," I said. "He might have stayed the night with one of them."

We genuinely missed the Arab. When he was with us, he would start up some topic or other, generally about what he had done during the day, about his experiences – some true, others concocted. Of the three of us the Arab was clearly the most knowing and worldly. Without the least interest in museums, old churches or monuments, he would regale us instead with his colourful experiences of night-clubs, dance halls and the like.

That night I was unable to get to sleep, although I made a pretence of it to enable the Brazilian to get on with his prayers. The basement seemed to be lying in a hush. The only sound was the rats behind the wallpaper.

"Are you sleeping?" The Brazilian's voice came through the darkness. I thought he was testing me. I lay still, holding my breath.

"Listen..." This time his voice struck a mildly anxious note, and I could no longer pretend sleep. "What's the matter?" I asked, turning on my side.

"Do you have any friends here?" he asked.

"No," I replied.

"Not even one?"

"No, not one."

We lay still for a while in the darkness.

"Why, what's the matter?" I asked him.

"No, it's nothing." The note of anxiety had gone from his voice now. He sounded composed and calm.

Turned on my side, I lay there facing the wall. The light of the lamp post filtering through the skylight fell palely on our boxes and beds. When someone passed along the road, his shadow moved like a slide projected on the opposite wall. For a long time we lay there shivering in the cold. In those nights I had often lain wondering which was more bearable – hunger or cold? Of course there was no point in speculating about such matters. We had no opportunity to choose between the two. We had to contend with both.

Then I also heard that pattering sound. I thought the Brazilian had gotten up and gone to ease himself. The toilet was two floors above, and we had to climb the stairs to reach it. But after a while I heard the same tapping, and I became suspicious. In the dark I groped my way to the Brazilian's bed and felt about for him. Lying on his stomach, he was deep in his slumbers. For a moment I thought it could be Monika tiptoeing on her paws. Monika was the cat that scratched on our door every night after meeting her lover. She would keep scratching until one of us opened the door and let her in to lie under a bed.

Groping my way through the dark, I opened the door. A hand fell on my shoulder, gripping it tightly. "Don't be afraid. It's me."

"You!"

"I've been banging on the door for the past half hour." In his hot, intoxicated breath the Arab's words fluttered like drying clothes.

"We thought you would not turn up, now that it's so late." I was now wide awake. The basement door was half ajar, and a cold wind had blown away my remaining sleep.

"Come in," I said.

But he just stood there holding my shoulder.

"Where's that Brazilian?" he asked at last.

"He's sleeping."

"Listen," he said, patting my shoulder. "You'll have to go out for a while."

"Outside? What do you mean?"

"There's a girl with me," he said.

So, here's something happening after all, I said to myself. Our days had been so uneventful.

"She's standing outside," the Arab said in a low voice. "I would like you to put on your clothes before she comes in."

I went in and sat down on my bed. He followed close at my heels. The basement door was ajar. "She's standing out in the cold," he said.

"I know," I said, without getting up.

"We met at a night-club. Later I invited her to come with me, and she agreed."

"But what about him?" I pointed towards the Brazilian.

"He will have to go out with you," the Arab said impatiently.

"But he's sleeping."

"Can't you wake him up?"

I felt like wrapping my blanket around me and going back to sleep. Having to go out in that cold was one thing, but what really jarred on me was the way he took things for granted, he seemed to be driving us out so easily.

I remained stock still, sitting on my bed.

"I'm not asking you to go out in the street," the Arab drew closer to me. "If you want, just close the door and stay in the vestibule."

"She's standing out in the cold," I said.

"What do you mean?" he said.

I started changing my clothes. He helped me to locate my things. It seemed he had never before taken so much trouble in helping someone else get dressed. I even misplaced some bits out of sheer cussedness; but I soon got bored with this game, with the darkness, with his breathing down my neck.

I was going to move out when he held me back by the hand. "Are you leaving him here?" he asked, pointing toward the Brazilian, who was fast asleep, ignorant of the drama being enacted around him.

"Let him sleep. He won't know anything."

For a while he stood there looking at me uncertainly, unable to decide how seriously he should take this suggestion of mine.

"I don't mind him so long as he's sleeping," he said at last. "But she may not be willing."

He had to make an effort to utter this sentence. He went to the other end of the basement and stood there with his back set against the wall. I had never seen such a strong and sturdy man give himself up so easily to despair. I walked up to the Brazilian's bed. A dim light filtering through the skylight was falling on his mother's photograph. I gently shook his shoulder, and before I could speak to him a rattling sound escaped his lips. His body was shaking.

I let go of his shoulder and switched on my flashlight to enable him to see my face. He quickly composed himself, and a faint smile flitted across his face.

"So you were trying to scare me, eh?" he said.

"We shall have to go out for a while," I said. "Outside the basement. Only for a short while."

His gaze travelled to the Arab, who was now

standing in the middle of the floor, watching the proceedings.

"When did you come?" the Brazilian asked cheerfully.

The Arab seemed to be at the end of his patience. He flung the Brazilian's coat on to his bed. "For God's sake, please hurry up," he said. "I can't keep watching this circus the whole night."

"What circus?" The Brazilian gave him a mystified look.

The door outside creaked. Then there was a gentle tap of feet as if someone was getting quite ill at ease outside.

"I think there is someone outside," the Brazilian said.

I held his hand and pulled him towards the door. In the darkness we could not see her clearly. But it was a girl all right, standing over the threshold.

The Brazilian stopped in his tracks. "I refuse to go," he said. That's the last straw, I thought to myself.

"Won't you go?" the Arab came up and stood behind him. He was breathing hard, as if he had just finished a long race.

"Why didn't you tell me before?" the Brazilian turned to me. But before I could have a word with him, the Arab gently pushed him towards the door. This caught the Brazilian unawares, and his head struck against the wall. He felt his forehead with his hand like a child to see if it was bleeding. To his disappointment, it was dry.

The girl was still standing at the door watching us intently. I found the situation rather comical. Here we were quarrelling like children before her. Leaving the Brazilian behind, I went to the landing. The next moment he came running to me. "You can't leave me alone like this," he said, panting.

"But I thought you wanted to stay."

"Son of a bitch!" he shrieked.

I dragged him to the basement door. For some time we stood there, peering into the darkness. It looked well-nigh impossible to go out in that freezing early November night. Fog was pressing against naked leafless trees, and a thin mist spread about us. The houses were very still, but if you looked at them steadily, they seemed to be floating like little paper boats.

"Who was that girl?" the Brazilian asked hesitantly.

"Could be any girl." I had started shivering. My hands and feet had turned numb with cold.

"Why has he sent us out?"

I looked at him and kept quiet. Was he pretending or did he really not know? Maybe I was pretending to understand the situation, just as he pretended to be ignorant of it. In a way, we were quits.

"In the rush I forgot to bring my gloves," he said.

"If you're feeling too cold we can still go in," I said. I myself wanted to go back but was reluctant to take the initiative.

There was a sharp click. The Brazilian gave me a surprised look. "The Arab has bolted the door from inside," he said.

"We can stand near the stairs," I said. "It's not so cold there."

It seemed my suggestion did not appeal to him. Perhaps he was right. The open street was at any time preferable to the darkness and stale air under the staircase.

"I don't suppose any restaurant would be open

now?" he said.

"At this hour?" I tried to give my words a touch of levity, but my effort misfired, and I ended up sounding miserable.

We came on to the sidewalk. The road lay deserted. The eerie stillness of an unknown city is not like the silence of one's own city. This thought struck me as odd somehow. But one is soundless, the other only silent. And silence has a familiar air about it. Before the world came into being there must have been a pervading stillness; when it comes to an end there will be silence. That was the only difference I could think of between the two.

"Do you know that girl?" the Brazilian asked me.

"No, I don't," I replied.

"Nor do I. I've never seen her before."

"The Arab met her in a night-club."

"How do you know?"

"He told me. You were asleep at the time."

"If we inform the Ministry, the Arab would be in big trouble," the Brazilian said. But there was no anger in his voice.

We stopped under a lamp post. There were old houses on both sides of the street, their windows closed and darkened. Sometimes a light would come on, and we could see a shadow behind a curtain. We would keep looking avidly at the shadow until the window merged into darkness again.

"Have you ever been out so late at night?" the Brazilian asked.

"Not in this city," I said, giving him a close look.

"I never stayed out so late even in my own city," he said. He was shivering from head to foot.

"You had no friends there?"

"Of course I had. But not like this Arab." He hesitated for an instant and then added in a whisper. "We don't entice girls like this."

"How do you know that the Arab has enticed her?"

"Didn't you notice how jittery she was looking?"

I looked at him. He must be around nineteen or twenty. Tall, dark-haired, fair-skinned, with an incipient beard and a dreamy sadness in his eyes which one finds only in boys who have never touched a girl.

We turned back and stopped in front of our building. There was no sound inside and no light. Climbing down the stairs, we stopped in front of the basement door. For some time we stood there, listening to the rats in the darkness. Every moment we expected some unspeakable thing to slither past our feet.

It was somewhat less cold here. But it was painful to know that we were so close to our beds and yet could not get to them.

"Won't you go in?" the Brazilian uttered the words as if I were preventing him from entering.

"She must still be inside," I said.

"If she stays here the whole night, do we then have to stand outside the whole night, too?"

"No, of course not," I said in a reassuring tone. But he refrained from knocking on the door and so did I.

After a while we heard a subdued noise inside, and our feet moved towards the door of their own accord. The latch clicked, but the door remained closed as before. I had a feeling someone was standing on the other side, as silent and expectant as we were.

I thought we should retrace our steps. But I could not stir from where I was standing. Tentatively the Brazilian gave the door a push and it flung open. We stood there transfixed. She was standing on the other side of the threshold, staring at us. She gave no impression of nerves. She was watching our discomfiture.

"Where's the toilet?" she asked in a low voice.

We stood there looking at her.

"Don't you people live here?"

The Brazilian nodded and so did I. She had recognised us.

"Can you tell me where's the toilet?" she repeated her question.

"Upstairs," the Brazilian said.

"Upstairs?"

I pointed towards the stairs, but it was quite dark, and one couldn't make out anything.

"Is there no light over here?"

"There's a light upstairs, but not on the stairs," I said.

The Brazilian lit his pocket flashlight and moved towards the stairs. It was the first time we were able to see the girl's face clearly. Her hair was dishevelled and was falling over her forehead. It appeared she had come straight from bed. Her forehead was narrow and there were blue hollows under her eyes, as if many sleepless nights had dissolved there. She glanced from one of us to the other. There was no fear in those eyes, nor any sense of shame or embarrassment: only a faint curiosity, which appeared out of place at that hour of the night.

"Please come with me," the Brazilian said. She looked at him and smiled. The Brazilian's face flushed, and he quickly climbed up the stairs, flashing his light. The girl followed, her hips rippling like the flanks of a horse.

Going into the room, I sat down on my bed. After the cold outside, the cold inside the basement felt almost pleasant. I fished out my pack of cigarettes from under the pillow. But my hand suddenly stopped. The Arab had turned on his side. I had completely forgotten about him.

"So you're back?" he said.

"Yes," I replied.

"May I have a cigarette?"

Going to his bed, I handed him the pack.

"Has she gone?"

"She's gone to the toilet. She should be back any moment."

The Arab started smoking. I proceeded to take off my shoes.

"Cold outside?" he asked. Despite the casualness of the question, there was a trace of concern in his voice. I liked that.

"Not bad," I said.

"I'm afraid she can't return to her hostel at this time of the night," he said.

"Does she live in a hostel?"

"That's what she told me. Maybe she lied to me."

Without removing my clothes I lay down on my bed. He might well ask us to go outside again. There were only three beds in the basement. There were more cots, but these were without mattresses – like hospital beds which are left bare for a time after a patient's death.

A blob of light on the wall grew larger. Then I saw the Brazilian standing at the door. He came near my bed and murmured to me, "Her name is Amalya."

"How do you know?"

"I told her my name and she told me hers." He was

breathing heavily.

"Amalya!" I was getting suspicious.

"She told me many more things but I could not follow her."

"What did she tell you?" I heard the Arab's voice in the dark.

The Brazilian gave a start. Like me he had also forgotten about the Arab's existence.

We heard a faint laugh at the door – a bright, cheerful laugh that seemed to have a separate existence from the darkness, and from the cold and smell of the basement.

She blinked at the flashlight's beam. She was standing on the threshold, holding Monika, who would scratch her paws on the door every night. Monika was resting her head against Amalya's neck.

"She was lying on the stairs," she said apologetically.

Sitting on our beds, we watched her steadily.

"May I bring the cat inside with me?"

The Arab growled. Was it at her or the cat? We could not decide.

For a while we couldn't tell where she was. It had started raining; and as we heard the patter of raindrops through the skylight, it sounded as if someone was boring small holes in the dark.

"What's this noise?" the girl asked.

"It's only the rats," the Brazilian replied.

"Rats?" the voice sounded scared.

"They generally avoid the basement," I said.

"Oh!" she heaved a sigh of relief.

"Are you afraid of rats?" the Arab asked in a bantering tone.

"I've a cat," she said.

The Brazilian and I were pleased with her answer. How witty of her! She had left the Arab speechless.

The Brazilian took out a half-burnt candle from his table drawer. He used it very sparingly. Burnt-down wax had collected at its base until it resembled a withered flower.

The candle threw only a dim light. But it did us good. It drove out darkness, brought in Amalya and drew us closer to one another.

"Whose photograph is this?" Emerging from a corner, she was now standing between our two beds.

"Your sweetheart?" she asked me brightly.

"No, she is his mother," I said, pointing towards the Brazilian.

She looked slightly disappointed and put the photograph back on the table. "Is it true?" she asked the Brazilian.

He nodded.

"I couldn't even imagine that someone could have such a young mother," she said. Holding the cat against her chest, she sat down on the edge of my bed. The light of the candle was falling on her face.

"You people live here alone?" She looked around, surveying the basement.

"There's an office upstairs. We live in this basement."

"For how long?"

"This is our fifth day," the Brazilian said. It was his favourite sentence. Only the number of the days varied, never the sentence structure.

"No, I wanted to know for how many more days will you be staying here?"

The Brazilian looked at me.

"We're waiting for our papers," I said.

"As soon as they are ready we shall leave this place," the Brazilian added.

"Him too?" she pointed towards the Arab, who was ensconced in his bed.

"Yes, him too," I said.

She fondled the cat. Her fingers were dirty. Under her fingers even Monika's fur looked white.

"Don't you people like to sleep?" She took us in with her gaze.

"We were sleeping before you came," I said.

"We don't need any more sleep," the Brazilian added, as if correcting me. "We can nap even in daytime." He had included me also in that "we".

"Don't you go stroll in the city during the day?" she said, feigning interest in us.

We did not answer her question.

"Maybe you have not liked the city much," she said.

"We don't know much about it yet," the Brazilian said.

"There's an old castle on top of the hill which all the tourists make a point to visit," the girl said.

"Have you been living here for many years?" I asked the girl.

"I was born here," the girl said, fondling the cat.

Her sense of informality had drawn me towards her. Gone was the nervousness which I had discerned on her face in the beginning. She was sitting with her legs drawn up, looking quite composed, as if she could never be surprised, as if she had known this basement and our niggardly condition for ages.

The Arab had dozed off and was snoring feebly. The girl looked at him.

"He's gone to sleep," she said in a soft voice, as if fearing he might be disturbed and waken.

The Arab having fallen asleep, we felt more at ease. We had even forgotten that only a short while ago the girl had been alone with him, and we had been shivering outside.

"Perhaps she's feeling cold," the Brazilian said to me.

She was indeed shivering. Except for the cat she had nothing which could lend her warmth.

"Haven't you brought your coat?" I asked the girl.

"Coat?" she laughed. "I left it in the bar. This friend of yours was in a big hurry and I was so drunk, I forgot I had a coat." She stretched the hem of her skirt over her knees.

We couldn't believe that she had come here drunk. In those days we thought that girls who drank belonged to a different breed, easily singled out from the others.

This was our fifth day in that city.

"This room of yours is cold. Don't you ever light a fire?"

"We may be moving out any day," I said. "Are you feeling chilly?"

"No, I'm all right. But..." she hesitated and looked at both of us in turn. "Don't you have anything to drink? I mean anything." She placed her hand on her stomach. "I'm feeling so empty and cold here."

The Brazilian looked at me. I was staring at the wall as if I had developed a sudden interest in the study of rats.

"I've got some coffee. Would you like to have coffee?" the Brazilian said.

I gave him a surprised look. He had never told us that he kept a stock of coffee handy.

The girl's face lit up. She lifted the cat and set it

down on the floor. "You mean you have Brazilian coffee?" she asked.

"Yes, I brought it from home. My mother gave me some when I was leaving." The Brazilian had suddenly brightened up.

"Where is it?" the girl gave the Brazilian an eager look. "We never see the real stuff here."

The Brazilian pulled out his suitcase from under his bed and, opening it, took out a packet of coffee. The girl snatched it from him and smelled it – once, twice, then fondled it as she had been fondling the cat. Her eyes had become dreamy.

"Once I met a Cuban," she said, "a writer. He took me to his hotel room and gave me a bottle of Cuban rum which he said I could take away with me. But the bottle was so big it wouldn't fit in my purse, and it was too risky to carry in out of the hotel in my hands. So I suggested we finish it off right there in his room. I didn't know the stuff was so strong. Just two glasses and I started feeling dizzy. But the Cuban kept on drinking and talking about Fidel Castro. I asked him if his Fidel could love me as he had loved me. He was furious and said that Fidel loved the entire world... So who'll make the coffee, you or me?" She looked at the Brazilian.

The Brazilian had been listening to her with rapt attention. The girl's world seemed to be magical, and we were peeping into it just by whisking aside a curtain.

"You won't be able to light the stove," the Brazilian said. "Let me prepare the coffee." Taking the packet from the girl's hand, he walked out swiftly. With great curiosity she watched him go.

"Your friend?" she asked me.

"Yes, we live here together," I replied.

"He's so childlike," the girl said thoughtfully. She took out a mirror from her purse and examined her face in it. Then she made up her eyebrows with a pencil and powdered her face. Her hand stopped while she was painting her lips, as if she had suddenly remembered something. She looked at the Arab, who was lying on his side, asleep as before. Looking relieved, she promptly put the mirror back in her purse and took from it a long, coloured scarf. She smoothed it out and covered her head with it.

"How does it look on me?" she turned to me and smiled. I watched her unblinkingly. Had it been some other occasion I would have told her that it looked wonderful on her. And it did indeed look nice. Some stray locks of hair escaped from under the scarf, making a dark outline on her forehead.

"You don't get such beautiful silk here," she said feeling the material between her dirty fingers. It seemed as if her fingers were made to have the feel of everything.

She removed the scarf from her head. "It cost five dollars," she said, dropping her voice to a whisper.

"You bought it here?" I asked.

"You don't get stuff like this here. He gave it to me," she pointed in the direction of the sleeping Arab. "He told me he had bought it for five dollars. She carefully folded the scarf and put it back in her purse. It was raining outside. She sat down on the Brazilian's bed with her knees folded up under the blanket and her head reclining against the pillow. She closed her eyes; and when she did not open them for some time, I thought she must be asleep.

I heard a faint noise outside the door and saw

Monika coming ahead of the Brazilian. Perhaps the smell of coffee had woken her up. The Brazilian stopped momentarily on seeing the girl on his bed.

The pale candle-light was falling on her face, sharpening the outlines of her dark eyebrows. She opened her eyes. "I'm on your bed," she said nonchalantly. "I hope you don't mind."

"No, I don't mind." The Brazilian's voice faltered. I took the kettle from him and placed it on the table next to the photograph. We had only one cup. After pouring the coffee into it, the Brazilian stood against the wall.

She held the cup between her palms as if warming her hands with it. I thought the Brazilian would make some conversation, but he stood mute. Six eyes were fixed on the girl – the Brazilian's, the cat's and mine. She didn't ask us once why we were sitting there staring.

"If the coffee's good, you don't need anything to go with it." She yawned, smacking her lips with satisfaction. She picked up the packet and looked at the Brazilian from the corner of her eye. "How much did it cost?" she asked him.

The Brazilian hesitated for an instant, looked at the girl uncertainly and said, "I don't know. My mother bought it for me."

The girl laughed. "If your mother got to know that I'm drinking your coffee, she might make a scene."

"She'll never know," the Brazilian said.

"Of course she won't." Amalya laughed and, holding his hand, pulled him towards her. The Brazilian made no move to resist. He only looked uncertainly in the direction of the Arab, who was lying on his stomach, fast asleep. The Brazilian sat down on the bed by her side. Monika had moved from under the bed and was lingering between their legs. She had long since given up the hope of getting any coffee, though the desire to keep herself warm was still there.

It was still raining outside. The girl looked around searchingly, steadying the cup of coffee on her knee.

"Your place is not bad," she said. "My room is much smaller."

"Do you live alone?" I asked her. We were gradually becoming informal.

"No, I share with another girl. She works in a bakery at night. When I go out to work I find her asleep and when she goes out to work she finds me asleep." She laughed and looked at us. "We can't meet each other except on Sundays."

"Have you got many friends here?" the Brazilian asked.

She was silent for a moment and then said in a sleepy voice, "Yes, I have friends and yet I don't have friends. Generally they are foreign tourists. Here today, gone tomorrow. But you people will be returning, no?"

"Maybe after a few months."

"They all say that," she said, looking at the candle flame with half-closed eyes. "If I meet them a second time I may not even recognise them."

"But I'll immediately recognise you," the Brazilian said with a tremor in his voice and his lips.

"Really?" She burst into a laugh. "But I won't be able to recognise you." She slid her fingers through the Brazilian's hair – dark, curly – which any girl would feel tempted to touch.

The Brazilian looked at her in dismay. "Are you sure you won't be able to recognise me?"

"I don't know. I feel very tired," she said. "I don't even know what I'm talking about."

Her voice had suddenly become soft like her fingers, which were gently moving through the Brazilian's hair. After a while I felt as if her words had dissolved in a spate of sounds, making it difficult to mark each word in its distinct individuality. Yet one could still see them like the mist floating on the opposite bank of the river. I had stayed awake the whole night, and everything seemed liquid to me, as if in a state of flux. I even seemed to forget that we were in our basement, three shadowy figures shrunk into themselves under the flickering candle-light. I was thinking of some other houses which I had not set eyes on for years. It seemed as if another being was within me whose presence I could feel, but only vaguely. And then there were moments when everything looked like molten glass, smooth yet jagged – the Arab lying in his bed and snoring in his sleep, the sound of Amalya's wobbly voice, the Brazilian's laboured breathing, muffled murmurs which sounded like neither the scurrying of rats nor the patter of rain. It was so pervasive that it seemed to have something to do with the basement itself and the darkness which had enveloped the whole of that unfamiliar city...

"Are you sleeping?" his head was bent over me.

I woke up confused. I had no idea how much time had passed. First I saw his forehead over which his curly hair was dangling. It amused me to see that he was still holding the cup of coffee in his hands.

"When did you come?" I had by now come out of the circle of blue fog and dark shadows.

Holding the cup, he continued to stare at me.

"Why are you standing over me?" I asked him. In

the dim, flickering candle-light his face took on a fearful look.

He kept staring at me. Then he said in a subdued voice, "She's thrown up – right on my bed!"

"On your bed?"

"She didn't even finish her coffee."

I could not decide what had upset him more – her leaving the coffee unfinished or vomiting on his bed. I looked around. She was nowhere to be seen.

"Is she gone?"

"No, she's standing at the door. She's afraid she may throw up again," the Brazilian said.

For a while we heard no sound except for the melting wax of the candle.

"She should get some sleep," I ventured.

"That's what I thought too," the Brazilian said eagerly. "Anyway, she can't go out in this rain. But..." He hesitated and trailed into silence.

"Yes, what's the matter now?" I prodded.

"My bed is not fit to sleep in," he said, his eyes fixed on the floor.

Now only my bed was good enough for her to use.

Both of us gave a startled look in the direction of the vestibule. Leaning against the door, Amalya was swaying from side to side as if standing on the deck of a ship.

"Let her sleep in my bed," I said.

"And what about you?"

"I'll stay out."

He looked at me steadily and then placed his hand on my shoulder. His hand was trembling.

"I don't want this." His voice seemed to be coming out of some deep hollow.

"The other alternative is that both of us should go

out," I said, "but that hardly makes sense."

"I feel all right now," Amalya gave a wan smile from where she was standing.

"Shall we call her in?" the Brazilian asked me quizzically.

But there was no need to call her. In she came, dragging her feet. White and yellow stains were clotted over her skirt. I shifted the blanket to enable her to lie down in comfort. She lay down and placed her head on the pillow. A colourless smile appeared on her face.

"I've spoilt your bed," she said gently, holding the Brazilian's hand.

"There's still some coffee left in the cup. Want it?"

She shook her head and stretched out her legs under the blanket. Her eyes were open, but she appeared to be asleep already.

I picked up my coat and muffler. The Brazilian caught hold of my hand. "I'll come with you," he said. His whole body was shaking, but I knew it was not from the cold. The shaking I am talking of a man experiences only once...and it is akin to the onrush of fever when the body falls apart from one's very being.

I pulled away my hand from his soft, trembling palms.

"That Arab..." he said in a faltering voice.

"Put out the candle," I tapped him on the arm and went out. Then I left the basement for the second time.

During our stay in the city that winter, all the days were not alike. Some were short, others shorter still, when the lamp-lights came on even before the afternoon was over. It was one of those short winter

days. I roamed about on the rain-drenched streets
throughout the hours of daylight. When the evening
darkness fell, I returned to my basement. There was
nobody there. I seemed to be having a slight
temperature. My teeth were chattering and as I
slipped under the blanket, everything looked hazy to
me.

Suddenly I felt as if someone was breathing over
me. It was like an animal's breathing, long-drawn,
heavy and rough. I just ignored it. I knew a man with a
fever can easily get things confused. But it was no
illusion. A candle was lit, and then the sound of
footsteps stopped near my bed.

"Were you asleep?" It was the Brazilian speaking. I
could make out his voice in the darkness even in my
delirium. The basement was palely lit by the candle.

"Are you all right?" he asked me.

"Yes, I'm all right."

"You were muttering in your sleep," he said.

I lay still. He brought a glass of water for me and sat
down at the foot of my bed.

"Hasn't the Arab returned?"

"No, not yet," he said.

I lay silent for some time. It seemed there was
something on his mind, but he could not bring himself
to the point of telling me about it.

"Didn't you go out today?" I asked him.

"Yes, I did," he said. "In fact, I was out the whole
day."

"Was she with you?" I gave him a smile.

He also smiled and shifted closer to me. "May I
bathe your head?"

"No, I'm all right."

We were talking in low tones as if there was

something very tender between us which we wanted to touch only with our silence and not with words.

"Do you know there's a river running in the middle of this city?" he said.

"A river? No, I didn't know." I looked up at him.

"I was myself not aware of it," he said.

"It's because you've been sleeping in a basement the whole day," I said.

He gave a faint laugh. I could not see his face. I had never heard him laugh.

"Yes, a river," he repeated in confirmation. "And many islands," he added. "I would not have known about these things if she had not taken me along with her. Do you know, I had not seen an island until now?"

"But you said you had spent some time in England," I said.

"I don't mean an island like that," he explained. "I mean an island right in the middle of a city – an island which you can see in its entirety at one glance."

"Was the Arab also with you?" I asked.

"No, we left before he woke up. She wanted to take me around the city before I left. We went to see the islands and then she took me to a restaurant. She asked me whether I preferred wine or vodka. I told her I did not touch liquor. Hearing this, she laughed. I felt embarrassed and ordered beer for us both."

"Did you have so much money to spend on her?"

"No, she wouldn't allow me to pay for anything. Listen, as a memento I gave her my packet of coffee. She had taken a fancy to it."

I turned on my side. He must have thought I was feeling tired. He lay down on his bed and put out the candle. In the winter night I could see the pantomime

of walking feet on the street above through
the skylight.

We lay in silence for some time.

"May I tell you something? You won't laugh, will
you?"

"No, I won't laugh."

"When you were gone I slept with her."

He heaved a sigh. A lifeless sigh which went
crawling over the silence of the basement.

I again turned on my side. My pillow had become
wet with perspiration.

"I slept with her. But I could do nothing," he said.

I could hear the sound of his breath rising over the
silence of the basement.

"Was it the first time that...?"

He blew his nose in his handkerchief. "Yes," he
murmured. "But I knew everything."

"It often happens like that the first time," I said.

"She also said the same," the Brazilian said.

"Who?"

"Amalya. She told me there was nothing to feel
embarrassed or afraid about. We can now sleep like
brother and sister, she said."

We lay in silence. We could make out the sky
through the skylight. The glow of the wintry night had
spread in the air. Some stray stars twinkled.

"May I light the candle? Just for a short while."

I thought he wanted to go to the toilet, but after
lighting the candle he came to my bed.

"I want to show you something," he said.

I looked at him. A bashful smile was peeping
through his moist eyes.

He fished out something from under his bedsheet
and placed it before me. I gaped at it.

"She gave it to me." He smiled.

I had recognised it at the first glance – the scarf said to have cost five dollars.

"What are you going to do with it?"

"I'll give it to my mother. She will be so pleased."

He carefully folded the scarf and placed it under his bedsheet. We again lay down in our beds after he had put out the candle.

"Don't show it to the Arab," I said.

"Why not?"

"No particular reason," I said.

I lay in bed listening to the scurrying of rats. In my fevered state the sound seemed to be so close and intimate. And then a long silence took over. Only once I heard a faint sound from the nearby bed – a subdued and listless sound coming from beyond the frontiers of somnolence. The Brazilian was standing before his mother's photograph, his head bowed in prayer – like every night. But not quite. For tonight something had come between him and his mother.

A river...and some islands scattered in the middle of the city.

The Visitor

He set his suitcase down by the front door, pressed the doorbell and waited. The house remained quiet; he could hear no movement inside. Perhaps there was no one home, he mused. Wiping away the perspiration with a handkerchief, he eased off his shoulder-bag on to the suitcase. He rang the bell again and pressed his ear against the door to listen: an open window at the end of the inner veranda swung in the wind.

He backed away into the street, looking up. It was a two-storey house similar to others in the lane: black gabled roof, grey outer stone wall, on its brow a circle around the house number, shining like a *bindi*. The upper windows were closed and the curtains drawn. Where could they have gone at this hour?

He walked round to the back of the house. The hedge, the lawn, and plants looked much the same as two years ago when he had last been here. A willow with dropping branches dozed in the middle like an old bear. The garage stood open and empty: perhaps they had just gone out on some errand after having waited for him since morning. But why had they not left a note for him at the door?

He made his way back to the front door, the August sun in his eyes. He sat down on his suitcase on the veranda. Before long he grew conscious of several pairs of eyes watching him. He looked up to see inquisitive faces leaning out of windows across the lane. He had heard that the English left strangers alone and did not intrude upon the privacy of others, but he was sitting out on the veranda where the word privacy had little meaning. In this small English town where everyone knew everyone else, he, an alien with rather odd looks and wearing an ill-fitting sagging suit, must surely attract attention. Nobody could have guessed from his crushed clothes and grimy, sweat-soaked appearance that only three days ago he had read a paper at a conference in Frankfurt. Probably they took him for a down-and-out Asian immigrant... He jumped to his feet. The door gave way. He heard footsteps on the stairs and saw his daughter come rushing down.

She came running and in another moment was in his arms, clinging to him. Before he could ask her if she had been in there all along or she could ask him if he had been waiting for ages, his sticky hands gripped her thin shoulders. The girl bent her head and he buried his face in her hair.

The neighbours withdrew.

The girl extricated herself gently. "Did you have to wait out here long?"

"Two years," he said.

"Oh!" The girl laughed. Her papa did frequently say bizarre things.

"I rang the bell twice. Nobody answered."

"It's not working, so I left the door unlocked."

"You could have warned me yesterday on the phone. I've been mooning around the house for an hour."

"I was going to when the line went dead. Why didn't you put in more coins?"

"I didn't have any except a miserable copper... That woman was a shrew."

"Which woman?" The girl picked up his bag.

"The switchboard operator who disconnected us."

He lugged his suitcase into the living room. The girl was looking into his bag expectantly. Cigarettes, Scotch whisky, Swiss chocolates: things he had bought in a hurry at the duty-free shops at Frankfurt Airport were now peeping out of his open bag.

"You have cut your hair short?" He held his daughter in a leisurely gaze.

"Well, so long as I have my vacation! How do I look, anyway?"

"If you were not my daughter, I'd say that a tramp had broken into the house."

"Oh Papa!" The girl burst out laughing. She took a chocolate and tore its wrapper foil. "Here," she said, holding it out to him on her palm, "a Swiss chocolate!"

"Can you get me a glass of water?"

"I have a better idea. I'll make you a cup of tea."

"Look, the tea can wait." He dipped into the inner pocket of his coat and out came his notebook, wallet, passport and lastly a pill-box. It was the pills he was looking for.

The girl returned with a glass of water. "What's that?" she asked, indicating the pill-box.

"It's a German medicine. Very effective." He swallowed a pill, washing it down with water, and settled back in an armchair. Everything around him was still the same as he remembered: the room with its glass-paned door, the lawn – small, squarish, quite green – beyond the curtains pulled aside, shadowy reflections on the TV screen of birds outside, casting their shadows within.

He went over to the kitchen. The girl stood there at the gas stove with her back to the door. She looked thin and frail in her white shirt over black corduroy jeans. Her sleeves rolled back above the elbows hung loosely.

"Isn't Mama home?" he asked. Perhaps his voice was too low, but he thought he noticed a light movement of her head. "Is Mama upstairs?" he asked again. Still, the girl gave no sign that she had heard. He knew then that she had heard him the first time. "Has she gone out somewhere?" he persisted. The girl shook her head slowly, vaguely. It could have meant anything.

"Will you please give me a hand, Papa?"

"What can I do for you?" He went into her eagerly.

"Take this teapot into the living room. I'll follow you."

"Is that all?" he said disappointed.

"All right. Take this tray instead – let me set it for you."

He took the tea-tray into the living room. He wanted to go back to his daughter in the kitchen but he was afraid to annoy her. An aroma of frying food emanated from the kitchen. She was obviously on her own and making a snack for him. He had half a mind to tell her he would eat nothing, but then realised he was starving. He had missed breakfast. At the cafeteria at Euston Station there was a long queue and he had just enough time to buy a ticket and get on the train. He thought he would order something from the dining car but later learned that it did not open until noon. In fact, the last meal he had eaten was at Frankfurt Airport the evening before. At night in his hotel in London he had taken out his book, thumbed through it, crossed over to the telephone booth and dialled the number. At first he was not sure whether it was his wife or his daughter at the other end. But the tense silence buzzing in his ears indicated that it was his wife. Then he heard her call out to their daughter. He glanced at his watch and it dawned on him that she must already be in bed upstairs. He was about to put down the receiver when he heard the child's sleepy voice. For quite some time she could not make out whether he was calling from India, Frankfurt or London. By the time he could explain his whereabouts, his three minutes were up and he had no more coins to feed into the slot. Anyway, he was glad that despite his sleepiness, alcoholic stupor and agitation, he had been able to put across to her that he would be in town to see them the next morning.

He was home now, sort of. Outside a soft pale sun filled the street of the small English town. A warmth surged through him. The panic that overtook him at airports or while checking in and out of hotels or rushing to meet train schedules was behind him. He was home, not his own any more, but a home nonetheless, complete with chairs, curtains, sofa, TV. He had lived among these things a long time long ago and the history of associations with each still clung to him. He would visit the house every two or three years. Each time he came wondering how big his daughter must have grown in the meantime, how the woman who was once his wife would have changed. Only the objects in the room remained unchanged.

They stayed with him wherever he went.

"Why don't you pour the tea, Papa?"

He looked up to see his daughter carrying two plates in her hands: toast and butter on one, fried sausages on the other.

"Come on, take it before it gets cold," she said, sitting down beside him on the sofa.

"I was waiting for you."

"Shall I turn on the TV?"

"No, don't bother. Listen, did you get the stamps I sent you?"

"Yes, Papa. Thanks. " She was buttering the toast.

"But you didn't write to me. Not even once."

"I did. But your cable arrived before I could post my letter. "

"You're a gaga girl!"

She looked up at him sharply and began to laugh as she recalled how he would tease her with nicknames when she was small and they all lived together – too small even to know that a country called India existed.

At once he seized the opportunity her laughter offered. He leaned forward over her as if she were an elusive sparrow that could be caught only in a moment of false security when its guard was dropped.

"When will Mama be back?" he shot the question at her.

It was too sudden for the girl to parry. "She is upstairs," she blurted.

"Upstairs, is it? But I thought you told me..."

Kirrach! Kirrach! The girl scraped off the burnt edges of the toast with a knife and with it, it seemed to him, his question as well. There was a smile like a dead frosted insect on her lips.

"Does she know that I am here?"

The girl finished spreading butter and jam on the toast and placed the plate before him.

"She knows."

"Won't she come down to have tea with us?"

The girl busied herself with rearranging sausages on the other plate. She got up abruptly, as if she had just remembered something. She went into the kitchen and returned with mustard and ketchup.

"I'll go up and ask her." He fixed on the girl to see how she took this suggestion. When the moment dragged on without her saying anything, he turned towards the stairs.

"Papa, please!"

He froze in his place.

"You want to kick up a row with Mama, do you?" The girl returned his gaze angrily.

"A row?" He grinned nervously. "Do you think I have come two thousand miles just to kick up a row?"

"Look, why don't you sit here with me?" the girl said in a thick voice. She was on her mother's side but not cruel to him, either. She looked up at him reassuringly, as much as to say: *I'm here with you. Isn't that enough?*

He began to eat his toast, sausage, processed peas. He had lost his appetite, but he ate under the girl's watchful eye. She nibbled at a piece of toast with a preoccupied air, a quiet smile on her lips, as if comforting him: *It's all right. I take you under my charge. You need have no fear so long as I am around.*

He had no fear. It could be the effect of the pill or sheer exhaustion of a long journey, but he wanted to be left alone at the moment. He wanted to escape from her eyes. "I'll take just a minute," he said, getting up to go to the bathroom. The girl looked at him suspiciously and followed him to the door. He shut it behind him. Still, it seemed to him the girl was hanging about.

He leaned forward until his face was in the bowl of the washbasin. He turned the tap. Water cascaded over his face with a hissing gurgle. Words unformed, unsaid, tore off like lumps of overgrown moss from the hollows of his heart. The pill he had swallowed a while ago, now half-digested, floated in a yellow curdled mess in the white enamel basin. He turned off the tap and dried his face on his handkerchief. His wife's clothes hung from a hook on the wall; her panties and bra were soaking in soapsuds in a wide plastic bucket. He looked out the window. The garden, which extended up to the bathroom, glistened in the bright sun. The sleepy purr of a lawn-mower in the neighbour's garden seemed to be drawing closer...

The house was quiet when he emerged. He looked into the kitchen, but the girl was not there. He retreated to the lonely living room. He suspected that she had gone upstairs to her mother. A terror gripped him: the quiet was all the more menacing. He went over to the corner to his suitcase. He threw it open almost in a frenzy. He turned over his conference notes and papers and took out from beneath them the presents bought in Delhi – a Rajasthani *lahanga* with its girlish sequins and embroidered skirt, blouse and headdress, bought from an emporium; zinc and bronze trinkets from a kerbside Tibetan hawker on the Janpath Road; the cashmere shawl for his daughter's mother; a pair of red brocaded velvet Gujarati slippers both daughter and mother could use; handloom bedcovers; an album of Indian postage stamps, and a large illustrated book entitled *Benares, The Eternal City*. In a short while the miniature India he carried with him every time he came to visit lay scattered on the floor about him.

His hands by his sides, he surveyed the dismal scene. The things lying pell-mell on the floor looked so pathetic. He had a mad thought to leave them lying there and run away. They would not even know where he had gone. The girl, of course, would be a little surprised, but then she was used to his sudden appearances and equally inexplicable departures. "You are a coming-and-going man," she used to say wistfully as a child and in later years in jest. She would not be unduly alarmed at not finding him in the room. She would go back to her mother to tell her he was gone. They would then come down together, side by side, relieved that they had the house to themselves again.

"Papa!"

He started as if caught red-handed. He smiled shamefacedly on seeing his daughter in the doorway. She was staring at his suitcase as though it were a magician's box that had produced all those colourful things on the floor. But her eyes reflected a sense of shame rather than pleasure, for she had readily seen through his trick. She feigned an exaggerated eagerness, however, in order to conceal her embarrassment.

"What a lot of things!" She dropped into a chair opposite him. "How did you get them through customs? They are very strict aren't they?"

"No, there was no problem, perhaps because I was coming in from Frankfurt. They had doubts about one thing, though," he said, smiling happily at the girl.

"And what was it?" The girl sounded

genuinely interested.

He took out a carton of *dalmoth*, a spicy mix of fried lentils, seeds and nuts from his bag, opened it and put it on the table before her. The girl hesitated before picking up three or four grains to smell.

"What is it?" she asked suspiciously.

"They also smelled it the same way." He laughed. "Perhaps they suspected that it contained hash."

"Hash?" The girl's eyes grew large. "Does it? Really?"

"Well, go ahead! Eat it and find out for yourself."

The girl placed a pinch of it on her tongue. She chewed cautiously but in a moment gasped loudly, a helpless bewildered look in her eyes.

"It's all that hot pepper. Spit it out!"

But the girl had already swallowed. She looked at him tearfully.

"You're crazy. Why did you have to swallow it all at once?" He made her drink water from the tumbler she had brought for him earlier.

"But I loved it." The girl gulped mouthfuls of water hastily. She wiped her eyes dry on her sleeve and smiled bravely at him. "I loved it," she repeated. She would say things just to spare his feelings. She knew she had very little time to spend with him, so she took shortcuts to reach him across the distance which other children take months to negotiate.

"Did they also taste it?"

"No, they didn't have your courage. They put it back in. As they turned over the papers on top, they realised I was returning from a conference, so they said: 'Mister, you may go.' "

"What! What did they say?" the girl cooed. "Did they say, 'Mister, you may go, like an Indian crow'?"

"Now, there! Wait a minute!" He threw the girl a searching glance. He recalled that when she was very young they used to go to a park. Often they played childhood games there. Looking up into a tree, he would ask her in mock earnestness, "Oh dear, is there anything to see?" She would pretend to peer all round before replying: "Yes, dear, there is a crow over the tree!" He would turn towards her in amazement. "What is it?" he would ask. "A poem," she would say triumphantly.

A poem! A memory of a lost childhood, of fresh park air and trees and laughter, swept up like a shadow across his jumbled years. Unwittingly, the girl had led him to a spot which she had herself walked out of long ago, but which recurred in his dreams every now and then.

"I've brought some Indian coins you wanted."

"Come on, let's have a look," the girl exaggerated.

He took out a red beadwork purse of the kind hippies carry their passport in. The girl almost snatched it from his hand, then shook and swung it in the air. The twenty-five and fifty *paisa* coins jangled in it. She released its top flap and turned it upside down, scattering the coins all over the table top.

"Does everyone in India have similar coins?"

"Of course! You wouldn't expect anyone to have his own mint, would you?" he said, laughing.

"But the poor – I saw them on TV once," she reflected, going off on a tangent. She cast an embarrassed glance at the objects on the floor. It struck him then that the girl now sitting opposite was not the one he had once known: this was a stranger. She still looked the same these two years later: the frame was familiar but the picture had changed. Yet it could be that the girl had not changed after all, only that she was momentarily preoccupied. Parents who do not live with their children know nothing about the stories that children construct on the foundations of their loss; they discover a world of their own to fill the empty spaces their parents leave behind. The girl could have met her papa only in the basement of her childhood, but right now she had drifted into other places, other rooms he knew nothing about.

"Papa, may I gather these things together and put them away?"

"What's the hurry?"

"If Mama comes down and sees all this..." She was worried and nervous, as if she smelled danger.

"What if she does?"

"Papa, please! Not so loudly." Her eyes turned towards the room above. Upstairs was utter silence. It occurred to him that the girl was playing her part in some mysterious puppet show: attached to invisible strings, she merely responded to the pull and jiggle of unseen hands.

He stood up abruptly. The girl glanced at him fearfully. "What are you up to, Papa?"

"Won't she come down?"

"She knows you're here." she said irritably.

"That's why she'll not come downstairs?"

"That's precisely why she can be here any moment. Can't you see? Listen, let me collect these things while you make yourself comfortable."

She squatted on her haunches with her back to him and began to pick up the things one by one to pile them in the corner. He could see her hands, thin and brown like her mother's, and equally distant and cold, which would not hold his intimate gifts even a moment but laid them aside indifferently. Those were the hands of a girl who had known only the tenderness of a mother, not the ache of a father's touch.

The girl stayed her hands at the ring of the telephone in the alcove under the stairs. It yelped like a pup straining at the end of its chain. The girl dropped the things in her hands and hurried over. In a moment she called out: "Mama, a call for you!"

The girl leaned on the banister, the receiver dangling from her hand. A door upstairs creaked open. The stairs shuddered as someone descended. A head appeared bent over the girl's upraised face, and the next moment, a full face, a woman's, came into view between a bun swinging low at the nape of her neck and the receiver held up in the girl's hand.

"Who is it?" the woman asked the girl, flicking the bun back over her nape. She took the receiver from the girl. He rose from his chair. The girl fixed him in her gaze. "Hello," the woman spoke into the phone. "Hello, hello!" she spoke louder. As her voice rose, he recognised it as his wife's. He would have known it anytime, anywhere, over the babble of a crowd. It trembled slightly at the higher pitch, hard, hurt and bewildered, a part of her that, wrenching itself free from her body, reached across his flesh to leave a furrow of blood on his soul. He dropped into his seat.

The girl smiled.

She was looking at his reflection in a wall mirror. He could see it was strangely distorted, warped, reversed, like the woman's mysterious voice in the mirror of age. The three of them had somehow grown into four, and split – the girl and her mother on one side, he and his wife on the other.

"Want to have a word with Jenny? She's on the line," the woman said to the girl, who jumped at once on to the upper step as if she had been waiting for just this moment to take the receiver. "Hello, Jenny, it's me."

The woman came down another two steps. He could now see her full-length. He stood up as she came near.

"Please, take a seat," he urged her, a note of desperation in his voice, lest she turn on her heels and go back to her room.

She stood there uncertainly. She realised finally that there was no point any more in turning back or continuing to stand about, and pulled a stool close to the television and sat down.

"When did you come?" Her voice was so low and remote that he thought he was hearing another woman speak in a telephone.

"It's been quite some time. I didn't know you were upstairs."

She looked at him in silence.

He wiped his sweat on his handkerchief and made an effort to smile. "I had to wait outside a long time. I didn't know the bell was out of order. The garage was empty, I thought the two of you had gone out... What's happened to your car, anyway?"

"I left it at the service station." She despised all small talk, but for him it was the proverbial straw to grasp at, for the time being anyway.

"Did you get my cable? I had my ticket extended in Frankfurt, where I stayed a couple of days. I tried to telephone you from there but perhaps neither of you was home."

"When was it?" She looked at him a little sceptically. "We've been home all these days."

"Well, the phone went on ringing: nobody answered. Maybe the operator did not understand my English and gave me a wrong number... Listen, a strange thing happened at Heathrow. I saw a woman there who looked just like you from behind. Thank God I didn't call out to her. All Indian women abroad look alike..." he went on and on. He was like a blindfolded man walking a high wire while the woman stood below, far below, in a dream. Why was he there at all? What for?

He fell silent. He realised he had been listening to his own voice all along. The woman had hardly spoken. She was staring at him with cold, despairing eyes.

"What's the matter?" he asked uneasily.

"Why don't you understand that I want nothing from you? Why do you bring all these things? What's the use?"

For a moment he did not catch on. What was she talking about? Then his eyes turned towards the corner – the Shantiniketan purse, the stamp album, the carton of *dalmoth*. These cluttered the corner, forlorn, beaten. "It's not much," he said defensively, "not even half a trunkful."

"But I want nothing from you. Can't you get this simple little notion clear?" Her voice rose, quavering, heavy with rancor, spilling over the dam that held back the anguished waters dark with memories of quarrels.

"Are even these short visits all that hard to stomach?"

"Yes, I can't stand them." Her face was taut. Suddenly it crumpled in sheer hopelessness. "I don't ever want to see you. That's all!"

Was it all that simple? He stared at her like a spoiled obstinate child, pretending he could not make any sense of it. "Bukku," he said slowly. "Please!"

"Don't!"

"What do you want?"

"Leave me alone. Is that too much to ask?"

"Can't I come even to see my daughter?"

"I'd rather you took her out."

"Out?" He stared dazedly at her. "Where?"

In that moment flitted across his mind the parks and streets and hotel rooms that were his lot in life. It was indeed a vast world out there, but where in it could he possibly drag his daughter?

He heard the girl's laughter. She was saying into the telephone, "No, I can't come today. Papa's here. He came this morning... No, I don't know. I didn't ask him." What didn't she know? Perhaps her friend had asked her how long her papa was going to say. Probably the woman who sat opposite him also wanted to know as much; she wanted to know how long, for how many hours yet, would she have to suffer the agony of his presence in the house.

The late afternoon sun slanted into the room. The TV screen caught its reflected glow. A shadowy image of the woman opposite reflected from its blankness, impersonal like a news commentator's. He waited for her to speak, although he was aware that their common past had produced only a tape, which relentlessly played out its document of pain every time they met. How different are material things from people! The house, the furniture, the books – these remain year after year as one had left them. These survive, unlike people, who begin to perish from the moment of parting. They don't really die; they just begin to live another life which gradually smothers the one they had once shared.

"It's not the girl alone," he stammered, "that I come to see. It's you as well."

"Me?" Astonishment and disdain washed over her face. She laughed sardonically. "You haven't quit lying, have you?"

"What would I get by lying?"

" *You* ought to know that. I know what I got, and I know I'm still paying for it." She stared out the window bleakly. "Had I known enough about you, I could have done something about it in time."

"What could you have done?" A cold shiver swept through him.

"Something. I can't live alone like you. But now, at my age, no one even looks at me."

"Listen, Bukku." He took her hand.

"Don't, please! It's all over."

She was weeping. Tears streamed down her face. She tried in vain to brush them away with her fingertips. Her tears did not seem to relate, not immediately anyway, to this man from her past or to any hope ahead. She seemed equidistant from both and all alone on the downward slope of years.

Their daughter was sitting on the bottom stair. She watched dry-eyed as her mother wept. All her effort had come to nought but she did not lose hope. Every family has its nightmares, which spin feverishly like a wheel within wheels and the girl knew better than to poke her hand in it: she knew that the wheel brooked no interference. Though young, she had already grasped the meaning of the parallel between one's inner universe and the outer: both shared a compulsive momentum; one could only wait for it to run its course.

The girl rose to her feet. She came across the room to her mother without a glance at the man, and spoke to her so softly that the mother pulled her down close beside her. They sat on the couch side by side like two sisters, oblivious of the man. The tidal wave which had engulfed the house a little while ago was retreating. It left him stranded where he ought to have been – on the beach. It was providential, he thought, that he had been granted in these few moments a lifelong wish to be invisible even as he sat with the two of them. God alone in His wisdom is invisible – this he had known. But a man who lived in a bottomless pit might also, he hoped, escape notice. The mother and the daughter took no notice of him, not to humiliate him though, just to let him be on his own.

At long last the girl moved over to him.

"Would you like to see our garden, Papa?"

"Now? At this time?" He stared at her uncomprehendingly. The girl looked impatient, as if she had something on her mind which she could not tell him about in her mother's presence.

"All right," he said, rising from his chair. "Move these things upstairs before we go."

"I'll do it later."

"What do you mean?" he asked suspiciously.

"Come on out, Papa!" The girl almost dragged him along.

"Tell him to take his things back." It was the woman's voice pitched high and harsh.

He stumbled, as if shoved violently from behind. He swung round. "That...what did you say?"

"I've no use for your things. Didn't you hear?"

A whirlwind stirred blindly within him. "I'll not take them back. You can throw them out if you like."

"I can throw you out along with them!" Her eyes washed by recent tears shone brightly.

"Come on, Papa, Let's go." He let the girl tow him out into the garden. He followed her in a daze. The lawn, the flower beds, the plants – all swam past as in an eerie silent movie. Only his wife's ghostly outburst ruffled the breeze: *I can throw you out too! Out! Out!*

"Why do you argue with Mama?"

"Do I?" He searched her face warily, as if she had also turned foe.

"You do," the girl insisted.

His heart stopped as a fear touched him like a cold finger. He could not bear to lose both his wife and daughter at the same time.

"It's a lovely garden you have," he flattered her. "Do you have a regular gardener?"

"No," the girl said, pleased with herself, "I water the plants myself in the afternoon and Mama mows and trims on holidays... Come with me, I'd like to show you something."

The girl led the way. It was a small lawn, green and velvety, with a hedge around it. In the middle stood the old willow. The girl disappeared behind it. Soon he heard her call out to him, "Where are you?"

He stepped round the tree and was surprised to see a black painted coop midway between willow and hedge. A rabbit was peeping out from behind its slatted shutter while another nestled in the girl's lap rounded like a ball of wool which threatened to slip out of her grasp and roll into the shrubs.

"We got these recently. As first we had two; now

there are four."

"Where are the others?"

"Here in the hutch. They are still too young."

He reached out towards the rabbit but his hand rested instead on the girl's head. His fingers played on the mop of her light-coloured hair. The girl stood still. The rabbit puckered its nose and gazed at her.

"Papa," the girl said without looking up, "did you buy a day return ticket?"

"No. Why do you ask?"

"Day return tickets are very cheap, you know."

Was this why she had dragged him out? His hand slid off her head.

"Where will you stay tonight?" she asked blandly.

"What if I stayed here?"

The girl let the rabbit into the hutch and slammed its door shut.

"I was joking," he said. "I'll go back tonight."

The girl turned to him and said very gently, "There are some good hotels here. I'll get you the addresses." Now that she knew he would not be spending the night here, she could break away from her mother to be with him. She took his hand and stroked it the way she had stroked the rabbit earlier. But his hand was clammy with perspiration.

"Listen, I'll come to India during my next vacation. I promise."

The rabbits scratched and squeaked in the hutch. He said nothing.

"Papa, why don't you say something?"

"You make that promise every time."

"I certainly will the next time. Believe me!"

"We'd better go in. Mama might be worried."

The August evening sky was darkening. The breeze

rustled in the willow. The curtains were drawn. The door to the kitchen was open. The girl went in to wash her hands at the sink. He followed her. There was a mirror above the sink. His face stared back out of it – grey, stubbled, red-eyed: *No, there is no hope for you.*

"Do you still talk to yourself, Papa?" Water beaded along her face as she looked up at his reflection in the mirror.

"Do I?" He placed both hands on the girl's shoulders. "Listen, do you have some soda in the fridge?"

"Sure. I'll bring it to you in the living room."

There was no one in the living room. All his presents had been gathered in a pile. His suitcase stood in the corner. While he was with the girl in the garden, his wife's eyes must have lingered on these objects, her hands must have reached out to touch them, to collect them together. Her anger towards him might be boundless, but the presents were a thing apart. She had not moved them upstairs, nor had she had the heart to put them back into his suitcase. She had simply left them to their fate.

In the gathering darkness he sat by himself, as if he were one of the fixtures. When the girl came in with soda and a glass, he could not for a moment recollect where he was.

"Why are you sitting in the dark, Papa?"

"I was going to turn on the lights," he said, getting up to look for the switch. In the meantime, the girl set down the tray and flicked on the switch of a lamp on the side table.

"Where is Mama?"

"She is taking her bath."

He pulled out the Scotch from his bag. As he poured himself a generous drink, he asked her, "What about your ginger ale?"

"I've graduated to real beer now," she said, laughing. "Do you want some ice?"

"No... Where are you off to?"

"To the bunnies. They like to have their food on time or they'll devour one another."

She went out. The open door gave on to a windless starlit night. Silence reigned out there; it filtered in through distantly familiar household sounds, lulling him into believing he was back home again. After ages, it seemed. She would be humming as she took a shower, and later when she emerged with a towel turbanned around her wet hair, water would drip a line across the floor. He did not know how or at what crossroads his hands had let go what he could never recover.

He tipped more whisky into his glass, although it was not yet empty. At this hour last night he was on the plane bound for London. He was drinking then, too. When the air-hostess announced that they were over the Channel, he looked out the window. But he could see nothing below except impenetrable darkness...dark flowing into another dark. As he peered hard he saw another Channel shimmer through the darkness within himself reaching from one end of his life to the other, which he was forever destined to shuttle across, back and forth, with the shore ahead not yet visible and the one behind already lost, belonging to neither, arriving nowhere.

"Where's Bindu?" He started at his wife's query, little realising that she had come in and was standing to one side below the banisters. "Out in the garden," he said. "Gone to feed the rabbits."

She had put on a robe after her bath. Her hair loose about her fresh glowing face, she looked calm, as if the shower had washed clean both her body and her anguish. She was quietly eyeing his drink on the side table.

"You can have some ice."

"No, thanks. This is all right. Shall I make you one?"

She gave a slight nod. He recalled how she liked to have a biting little drink after a hot bath. He had not forgotten her likings yet. Indeed, it was memories such as these, trivial ones perhaps, which still served to bridge the distance between them. He went into the kitchen to fetch a glass and ice cubes. Even as he poured a tot for her on the rocks, she called out softly, "That's enough. Thanks."

It was a clean voice, washed of any touch of resentment or affection – cool, collected, detached. She approached him across the room.

She accepted the drink from him and pulled an ottoman to sit down near the television, out of the circle of lamplight.

"How is everybody back home?" she inquired after a while.

"Fine. They sent you all those things."

"But," she said wearily, "it's not fair to bother them."

"The pleasure is theirs. They remember you often. You haven't been to see them even once in all these years."

"What's the use?" She took a long sip from her glass. "We're no longer related."

"But you could accompany Bindu to India, couldn't

you? She's never even seen the country."

She did not speak for a long, long while. Then she said slowly, thoughtfully, "She will be fourteen next year, when she can – legally – go anywhere she likes."

"I was not talking of legal rights. She will not go anywhere without you."

She studied him over the rim of her glass. "I'll not send her to India, ever, if I have my way."

"Why do you say that?"

She laughed in a tired sort of way. "Don't you think she's had enough of India between the two of us?"

He made no answer; there was nothing he could say.

Before long, the girl returned from the garden. She looked at them quietly before going to the telephone.

"Who are you calling?" the woman asked her.

The girl preferred not to reply. She continued dialling the number. The man got up. "Would you like to have another small one?" he asked the woman.

"No thanks," she shook her head.

The man poured himself, slowly, a stiff drink.

"Do you drink a lot these days?"

"No," he said, shaking his head, "not unless I'm travelling."

"I'd expected you'd have set up a home by now."

"How come?" He stared at her. "What made you think so?"

She examined him with expressionless eyes. "Why, what happened to that woman? Doesn't she live with you any longer?" There was no trace of agitation or bitterness in her voice. She talked calmly of an event which long ago had flung them apart on distant shores at one stroke.

"I live alone with Mother."

"What went wrong?" She was obviously surprised.

"I don't know. Perhaps I'm too difficult to live with," he said in an undertone, as if he were talking of some brothel disease rather than his loneliness. "You're surprised, aren't you? There are some people who..."

He wanted to talk of something else though – of love, loyalty, trust, betrayal, of some great truth compounded from several small lies, something which flickered across the haze of whisky like lightning before flashing into the darkness forever.

Meanwhile, the girl had finished telephoning. She crossed the room and glanced up at her mother, who sat back in the half-light. And he? He was a mass of jelly, a mere smudge, behind his glass.

"Papa," the girl held out a slip of paper to him, "here is the address. A taxi will take you to the hotel in ten minutes."

He pulled the girl down beside him and took the slip from her. They sat beside each other in silence. Outside, countless stars shone in the sky. In their feeble light the old willow, the bushes and the rabbit hutch seemed to huddle closer together.

He set his glass down on the table. He kissed the girl gently. Then he picked up his suitcase. The girl opened the door. He hesitated in the doorway. "Well, goodbye!" he said, without turning round. He wasn't sure whom he had spoken to, but no sound came from the corner where she sat on the ottoman. There was silence as thick as the darkness into which he was going.

The Gossamer

After dinner my elder sister and I were having coffee in her living room when the conversation turned to the records of classical music that Keshi, her architect husband, had bought earlier in the day. I'd once asked Keshi how he, an architect, could be so fond of music, and he said, "There is space there." I must have looked puzzled, for he added with a self-conscious smile on his lips and a strange faraway look in his eyes, "You see, both architecture and music probe space in their own way."

"I've removed the record player to Keshi's study," said Meenu. "I couldn't sleep with that thing going on and on so close to our bed."

"Does he still drink?"

"Yes, he does – but in his study."

Meenu got up, drew the curtain aside, slipped the bolts and pulled open the grille-panelled door to the veranda. Beyond it the lawn lay submerged in darkness. A deep silence stretched from the hedge across the lawn to the doorsteps and spilled into the living room.

We dallied over our by now empty cups. Meenu pulled a chair beside me.

"Your hands are so cold, Rooni," she said, taking both my hands in hers. She turned them over, palms up. "Tell me, Rooni, why were you so late tonight? Shaila waited up for you till she dropped off to sleep."

I didn't have the heart to tell her I'd been out there on the dark lawn sitting by myself for half an hour before I knocked on her door. Nor would she have believed me had I told her the truth.

Her hand slid down on my lap. It looked so bony, so pale in the electric light. How, I wondered, could Keshi ever bring himself to kiss it or stroke its tawny down?

"Look, what were you doing the night before last?"

"I was in my room," I said.

"We stopped by your hostel on our way back from Connaught Place."

"You're kidding."

"You can ask Keshi if you like. We didn't go in to see you; it was much too late for visitors and we were afraid Mrs Harry would jump on us," she said with a laugh. "The light in your room was on. Keshi honked several times to draw your attention, but perhaps you didn't hear it."

"I might have been asleep."

"Do you still sleep with the light on? Doesn't Mrs Harry object?"

"It's a working women's hostel. Mrs Harry isn't a matron in a convent school, is she?"

Meenu started laughing, and I with her, as it flashed across my mind how, as a schoolgirl scared of darkness, I had often pleaded with the matron doing her bedtime rounds of the dormitories to let me keep the light on. The other girls used to tug at my frock, mimicking me: "Please, Matron! Please!"

"Rooni," Meenu said hesitantly, "we've been thinking of going to Simla for a short holiday. Couldn't you come along?"

I stared at her blankly.

"Don't you see what you're doing to yourself, Rooni? Haven't you looked into the mirror lately?"

"It's a lovely face I see in the mirror."

"Come off it, Rooni – don't be silly. You must go with us. Ever since you've come back from Jabalpur..." Her sentence trailed off into an embarrassed silence as she saw the colour drain from my face.

Meenu came over and put her arms round my neck. I had a sudden feeling that she knew everything there was – there had been – between Keshi and me. She knew all that I'd kept carefully even from myself. But she wouldn't speak of it to me. Being the elder, she would play the martyr. Oh, how I hated that!

"I've hurt you, haven't I?"

"You're crazy, Meenu."

"But how long can you go on staying at the hostel?"

"I'm no longer afraid," I said with a grin.

Meenu ran her fingers through my hair distractedly. She looked so sad.

A pale sliver of moonlight had descended to the grille in the door. Out there, beyond the veranda, was an ochre gravelled driveway, and, in the distance, a rocky hill overlooking the main road. A light breeze shuffle through the grass on the lawn and swished the dry leaves about.

"Come, get up, Rooni – it's time for bed."

"Those bushes on the hill over there must be laden with berries by now, aren't they?"

"The berries won't be ripe until December. Don't you remember, it was about this time last year we went picnicking on the hill; and Shaila ate those raw berries and got sick?"

"But the ripe ones are sweet as strawberries. You remember we used to eat them at Simla?"

"And the sour pomegranate," said Meenu. "You'd scare Mother by staining your fingers with its red juice and pretending it was blood."

In that instant, we seemed to have cast aside the mound of years that had grown over us since our childhood. We were no longer aware that Meenu had married several years ago and that I was myself the mother of a daughter. We stood in the doorway reminding each other of what we nevertheless remembered well, of what we in fact repeated to each other often, not to forget.

"We'll go for a picnic on the hill tomorrow. What do you say?"

"Shall we really?" I was so pleased I squeezed Meenu's hand.

"We'll ask Keshi to take his tape recorder along, and we'll have a great time like last year."

The memory of last year sent a shiver down my spine. I had come to Delhi with Shaila for good, leaving behind hearth and home. Everybody here took it for granted that I would go back in a few days, so I decided to tell Meenu. It was September then too, and we had gone to the hill for a picnic. When I found Meenu alone behind a bush, I had taken courage and made a clean breast of it. At first she had thought I was joking, but when she saw the look in my eyes, her mouth hung open in horror.

The light was still on in the guest room. I turned round at the door and looked across the lawn. My shadow sprawled behind me in the clear moonlight.

The grass was dark under the plants and where the shadows overlapped.

I could see the outer part of the corner of the master bedroom; Meenu and Keshi slept in there. The shadows of the plants slouched close to the wall. Suddenly it struck me that I knew that house much too well and shouldn't come here any more.

At last, I turned to go in. Shaila lay in the bed next to mine. I took my *chappals* off my feet and went to the edge of her bed, looking long at her closed eyelids. She opened her eyes, but sleep drew her back into its warm folds.

Switching off the light, I lay down on my bed. The moonlight picked out the title on the dust jacket of Keshi's *Time, Space and Architecture*. Shaila's swing was slung over the open window, and its cords threw slanting shadows across the window screens. The shadows jumped closer together and shivered, as if frightened by a rising wind.

Without warning, my heart began to pound. I could have been mistaken, but I thought I heard faint footsteps in the passage. A warmth crept from the walls around my bed and mingled with the breathless dark silence. I felt hot.

I tried to listen as attentively as I could. Some tense moments later, the faint sound in the passage came again. So it hadn't been a delusion after all. I waited with bated breath. The outer door creaked open, and closed again, as the breeze swirled the dusty leaves in the passage like moths up against the wall.

The light in Keshi's study across the passage came on. After some hesitation, I took Meenu's shawl off its hook, threw it over my shoulders and went out barefoot. The door to the study was open. Keshi's face was hidden behind the green lampshade, but his legs stuck out in front of the sofa. A bottle of cognac and a glass stood on a tripod, and his record player was on another table beside him. Their shadows made a still life on the wall behind Keshi.

"Well! Couldn't you go to sleep?" Keshi asked me as I stood in the doorway.

"What are you doing here so late?"

Keshi sat up, his finger stuck in the book he was reading.

"Nothing in particular. Just the usual drink and a bit of reading. I don't like to disturb Meenu, you see."

"Do you sleep here?" My voice sounded strange and unfamiliar even to my ears.

"Sometimes," he said. "Anyway, it hardly makes a difference, does it?" He gave a short deprecatory laugh.

Outside, leaves scampered on the pathway across the lawn.

"I looked in at your room before coming here. I thought you were asleep."

"Did you have something to say to me?"

"Won't you sit down, Please?" Keshi looked impassive; his expression gave nothing away. "There's a letter from Jabalpur," he said. He took an envelope from his pocket and laid it on the record player in front of him without meeting my eyes.

I recognised the writing on the envelope, and saw again the face of the man who wrote it. Would I never be able to get rid of my past? Would its long shadow always pursue me? I couldn't bring myself to reach for the envelope.

"Won't you read it? I wanted to ask you what to write to him." Keshi looked up at me desperately. "He wants you to come back to him."

"I know."

"He wants to see Shaila."

"He is Shaila's father. He can come anytime. He can even take her away. I won't stop him."

Keshi stared out the window. It was a long time before he spoke: "What have you decided for yourself, Rooni? What are you going to do?"

I looked at him in spite of myself. Keshi couldn't see inside me, could he? If he could, he'd have seen how vulnerable I was, how helpless. In his matter-of-fact manner there was nothing that could lend me strength... All of a sudden, I was ashamed of myself. I burst out laughing at my weakness.

"Rooni!" Keshi's voice sounded strange from his dry throat; and his face paled, choking my laughter.

"I've nothing more to say to you. You can go to your room."

I stared at his open collar; I saw the pale brown hair on his chest, and I heard Shaila breathing quietly in her sleep in the nearby room. It was a reassuring sound. I pulled myself together.

"I hear you bought yourself some records today."

"Oh yes, I did. Want me to play one for you?"

"Not now. It's too late."

"We passed by your hostel last night."

"I know – Meenu told me. And you hooted your horn."

"Did you hear it? Why didn't you come out? We waited on the porch quite some time."

"I was asleep then. I thought I heard your horn in my sleep."

Silence fell between us again. We were like two travellers thrown together in the waiting room of a remote railway station. We couldn't help but wait for our trains, and try to pass the time pleasantly, so that neither might have anything to regret later.

"You won't mind, Rooni, will you?" Keshi said, reaching out for the bottle of cognac. I nodded like a good sport.

I watched him lean forward to drink. There was something elusive about him. I looked at his round pale face, prominent cheekbones, sad eyes, and the wide forehead below the receding hair-line. There are some faces which leave an instant impression, I told myself; but there was nothing of the sort in Keshi's, nothing that startled, nothing that held one's glance.

"I saw you sitting on the lawn this evening," he said.

"Did you?"

"You were sitting in the dark. I'd seen you come through the gate. It was dark, and you sat down on the grass. No one else in the house noticed. They kept waiting for you, and all the while you sat out there in the darkness." Keshi wasn't looking at me. He was looking out the window, as if I was still there on the lawn.

He refilled his glass, though it wasn't empty.

"We might go to Simla for a few days," he said.

"I know. Meenu told me."

"Will you come along?"

I laughed it away.

Dry leaves scraped along the passage. The outer door creaked on its hinges.

"Look here, Keshi," I said. "Would you mind if I asked why you wanted to show the letter to me? Did you think I'd go back?"

"It's up to you, Rooni."

"But would you rather I did?" I choked on my

words as I realised we were beyond their comfort. Words had lost their meaning for us: we might as well lie and be none the better for it.

Keshi picked up his glass slowly. A spot of light floated on the cognac in his hand.

"How long can you live in a hostel, after all?"

"Since when have you started feeling so concerned about me, Keshi?" I said recklessly.

Keshi's forehead glistened with a thin patina of moisture and his eyes stared into his glass.

I told myself then I must get up and go to my room, but I kept on sitting. It occurred to me vaguely it might look strange if anyone saw me alone with Keshi so late at night while Meenu was in her bed asleep and Shaila was also sleeping in another room. How happy and surprised the girl would be to find me beside her in the morning, and I was happy too: I'd be gone the next evening to Mrs Harry and my lonely hostel room, safely out of the way of this bungalow, and Keshi's record player, and the letter on the record player, and the many questions I couldn't answer.

There was a faraway distracted look in Keshi's eyes. I'd seen it before, as a child at the Sanjauli cemetery in Simla, in the eyes of an old Englishman who had prevented us from going in to see the graves. Hills rose all around the cemetery, and rocks, and tall grass among the rocks. I was accompanied by our servant. We were standing at the closed gate when the old man saw us and came over. "Why is the gate closed?" I asked him. "It's always closed," he'd said with a smile on his lips and a strange distant look in his eyes, "so that the dead may lie in peace." That inviolate look was there now in Keshi's eyes; and I saw a closed gate and graves and rocks and a breeze bending the tall grass, and I told myself I really must get up...

I retreated to my room across the passage and lay down on my bed. I could hear the crickets chirp out there on the lawn. The curtain rings gleamed in the moonlight, and when the breeze played upon them they tinkled gently.

A long while afterwards the light in Keshi's room was still on and a bar of light splayed out through the partly open door. Outside, the moon shone sound-lessly on the bushes, the housetops, the hill beyond. Over there among the ancient rocks was a berry bush where last year I'd found Meenu alone and where my words had tumbled out. No one knew, nor ever would, that those words still lay in the dust with unripe berries under the bush.

I woke in the dead of night, frightened perhaps by the shadows of the swing in the window. I wanted to push away the top sheet but my terrified hands hovered inert in the darkness and my legs went cold. I looked at Shaila asleep in her bed with the coverlet drawn over half her face. Wan moonlight rippled over the other half.

I got out of my bed and went over to the door. I looked out into the dark passage: the light in Keshi's room had been turned off but his door was still ajar.

I crept to my doorway.

There was a sound, a stream – no, a cascade of sound rising even as it fell in a thin mist of spray, thinner than air, shimmering, heaving like a lover's breath, and falling gently; gently it rolled down to me and no one stopped it; no one could stop it. It fell, heavy with itself. But then it seemed to be sucked into a whirlwind: a trapped spiral of air, with wings beating frantically in a desperate bid to escape...

"Keshi," I spoke to myself. "Keshi," I whispered again, standing there in the dark doorway. And there was a dark cloud inside me, rolling, churning, breaking into a ceaseless, drenching rain.

It must have been one of the records he'd bought. He would have no rest until he had played all the new ones.

I turned to Shaila. My hand reached out under her pillow and I moved into her bed, seeking the warmth of her young body.

I looked about me in the dark room. In a pale sliver of moonlight, my eyes came to rest on Keshi's *Time, Space and Architecture*. As I dozed off I thought vaguely of space and of the next morning and the picnic on the hill, and I saw again a closed gate and the tall grass among the rocks and a breeze in the grass whispering gently to me to let the dead lie in peace...

Last Summer

Nindi stood in his trunks on the bottom step of the swimming pool. His toes arched forward into the water, and the pleasant sensation rose through his body. He longed to let himself go. His eye skimmed the surface of the pool, blue, calm and drowsy in the bright summer sunshine.

Unable to hold himself back any longer, he jumped in.

He went to the swimming pool often during those Delhi summer days. He would spend whole afternoons in its cool aquamarine, drifting in a blissful haze, home and the city thrust way to the back of his mind.

When he surfaced this time, he saw Mahip waving from where he had come to sit on the grass by the pool. Behind him, the last rays of the sun shone on the whitewashed clubhouse.

"Enough!" Mahip shouted. "Come, let's go in for a drink."

"Wouldn't you like to have a swim?"

"No thanks. I'm too thirsty," Mahip joked. "Hurry up – you're keeping me waiting."

He wanted to stay in the pool – how he wished he could soak there overnight! The electric lamp-globes switched on around the pool in anticipation of dusk. He began to scrub himself with a towel.

"Don't you get fed up?"

"With what?"

"I can't stand the water for more than five minutes."

Nindi peeled off his wet swimsuit.

"What a shameless boor you are!" Mahip snorted, looking away and red in the face.

Nindi burst into laughter. He had a great desire to jump right back into the pool – naked. How glorious that must feel, he mused.

Presently, however, they walked over to the lounge. After a good splash there's nothing like a beer, he told himself, especially if it is well-chilled and you have nothing else to do. Indeed, he had had nothing to do for several days. He was home on vacation for the first time in three years from his architectural studies in Vienna.

"Any news from Keshi?" Mahip asked.

"None," he said. "It seems he may not make it." Keshi was his younger brother.

"Aren't you going to see him before you leave?"

"I don't know – it all depends."

He looked at Mahip, sipping his beer in silence. He had known several of Keshi's friends, but it was Mahip he had sought out on his return. He had had very few friends of his own, and even they had moved closer to Keshi over the years.

"You haven't already finalised your plans for the return flight by any chance, have you?"

Nindi tipped the rest of the beer into his mug. "There's time yet for everything," he drawled. He had long since stopped keeping track of the days. Earlier, much earlier, he used to await each day; and each new day then had the sparkle of smooth clean pebbles at the bottom of a clear pool. But now the lustreless pebbles rolled by, unlooked for and unnoticed.

"I'm going to get another bottle," Mahip said. "What about you?"

"We could share it."

"Those beer gardens in Vienna. You go there often, don't you?"

"No, I don't – believe me. But they're open in the summer, and they have outdoor orchestras." Even as he spoke he could see that Mahip was not really interested. Had Keshi been here, Mahip and his brother would have made lively conversation while he himself would have been content with listening. Keshi's absence seemed to have made Mahip conscious of a certain obligation towards him, which expressed itself in talk for its own sake. Many a time Nindi had tried to impress upon Mahip that he didn't have to keep the conversation going, that his mere presence was enough. But Mahip would have none of it.

Outside, it had grown dark.

"How can you stand it, day in day out, inside the four walls of your room? I don't understand it," Mahip struck out at a tangent.

"It's all right – I don't mind it."

"It seems you feel rather out of place here. Isn't that so?"

"Well," he said, lighting a cigarette, "sort of." His own words sounded strange to his ears. He was glad Mahip could not see his face in the darkness.

"Things'll work out if you settle down here. You only have to make up your mind."

"I haven't given it a thought." Some years ago he had given it more than a thought; he used to be keen then. Later, he had learned to scoff at his enthusiasm.

They walked out of the lounge into the open. Nindi felt the breeze of the August evening through his still wet hair. He had always liked August in Delhi, for it was so unobtrusive you had the freedom to think of days gone by or days to come – a bridge that straddled an airy nothing, yet provided safe passage.

They reached Kushak Road across Willingdon Crescent. A gust of still quite hot wind swept the dust on the footpath up into the overhanging rose-apple branches to settle on plants on the other side of the hedge. Nindi had lived in this part of the city many years ago with his parents, little Keshi and their elder sister Neeta. His father was not retired then. He recalled how they used to sleep out on the lawn at night while the sagging badminton net fluttered noisily in the wind. Neeta would sometimes wake up crying, frightened perhaps by a bad dream or the creaking of the net. Nindi wanted to share some of these memories with Mahip but refrained for fear Mahip would think the beer had gone to his head. At a time like this, he told himself, Keshi would have kept his mouth shut. He used to say that if you started dredging up the past when you're mellow, you lacked deep feelings.

But he did think he lacked deep feelings. Perhaps it had been different when he was young. He recollected saying to Keshi one night: "I'm dying." He was very small then. Keshi was thoroughly impressed. Many years later Keshi told him: "If you'd died that day I'd have been sad, but I'd have got over it. You said you were dying but you didn't – this showed the depth of your feelings."

They came to a stop in front of the Secretariat.

Many buses were lined up, but not Mahip's.

Mahip took a deep breath. "Did you call on Aruna?" he asked point-blank.

"No."

"If all you wanted was to hole-up in your room, what was the point in coming all the way back here?"

"There's time yet," Nindi said evasively. He looked away at the old barracks. This summer he had felt people were giving him puzzled looks. They said nothing, of course, and he could have been wrong; it could as well have been his own imagination playing tricks on him, particularly after he had had a couple of drinks.

Mahip's bus pulled in. He hopped on board.

"See you tomorrow evening at the pool!" he called out.

"I'll be there."

The bus pulled away, leaving Nindi alone.

Nindi got back home late every night, but his father didn't take it amiss. On the contrary, he only worried that his son was spending too long about the house. Nindi, for his part, wanted to reassure his father that he was happy. Indeed, years later, he did think he had known happiness that summer, but he couldn't have told anyone so. If he had said he was happy, nobody would have believed it. Indeed, he might have set himself up for ridicule.

Nindi had nothing to do all day long. Because Keshi, who had joined the army, was away with his unit, he spent his days alone in the rooftop room until it was time to go to the swimming pool. He preferred to spend as much time as possible at the pool. Not that he didn't like his home well enough – he did; but it was depressing to face his aged and lonely parents for whom he could do nothing.

When he thought his father had gone to sleep, he settled down on his bed with a cognac. A couple of times his mother had caught him at it, but she had said nothing. He didn't like her saying nothing.

He was going quietly up the stairs to his room one night when he overheard his parents. He was a little surprised that they were talking about him.

"Do you know how he spends his day? I can't say I see much of him." It was his father.

"You worry too much," his mother said. "He's young. He's come back after three years abroad. He wants to be on his own. So what's wrong with that?"

"No, I didn't mean that." His father sounded confused and embarrassed.

Nindi hurried up the stairs.

It was a relief to be up on the terrace. He had brought several paint and whitewash cans and brushes up there. He stood a creaking ladder against the plastered wall of his room and roped a can to a rung. As the moon rose overhead, he could see more clearly. Paintbrush in hand, he forgot how late it was or that his mother must be waiting downstairs with his food. He clung to the ladder like a bat while his shadow bulged under him, a misshapen animal.

On those sweaty August nights Nindi painted the walls of his room, tidily, tastefully. As he perched atop the ladder, the infinite space over the Delhi skyline, crossed by the wind, stirred in the pit of his stomach. The wonder of the moonlit night out in the open, like blue waters kneading the hollows in his limbs, left behind an aching, utter calm.

At last, when he got down from the ladder, he saw

his mother standing in a shadow, watching. Shy and
retiring, she became self-conscious under his gaze.

"When did you come, Mother?"

"I didn't find you in your room, so I came here."
She was a small woman, grown smaller with age.
Small and shrunken. "Aren't you hungry yet?"

He put away the dripping brush and the lime can in
a corner and laid the ladder flat along the wall. "I'll
take just a minute," he said.

His mother, Nindi noticed, had been behaving
rather curiously of late. The first few days of his visit
she was cheerful and effusive, but now that his
vacation was drawing to an end she had withdrawn
into her shell. The little she spoke had an undercur-
rent of apprehension, and mostly she repeated herself.
She had borne with studied silence his departure three
years ago. Now, too, she kept her thoughts to herself
even as he prepared to go away again.

They often ate dinner together. His mother squatted
cross-legged on a mat and his father on a divan beside
the radio on a table between two empty chairs
– Neeta's and Keshi's. Neeta had married, and Keshi
was in the army. The sight of those two empty chairs
never failed to make Nindi feel lonely.

Over dinner, his father had once asked him with a
tentative smile, looking away in the direction of his
mother: "You don't get these things to eat there,
do you?"

Food was something that interested his mother.
"Neeta says that all one gets to eat there is fish or
meat or things like that. Is that so?"

Another time his father queried: "Isn't it very cold
over there?"

"It's cold, yes. But the houses have central heating."

Dinner over, Mother left to look after her nightly chores, and fraught silence fell between father and son. After the sharp break of three years, they were at a loss for words. Outside, the moonlit, hot summer night seemed to have closed in around the house. Nindi waited for his father to speak, but his father fixed an expressionless gaze on him and remained silent. Nindi's shirt was damp under the armpits with sweat. He prayed inwardly for Father to speak his mind and defuse the tension that had built up between them over the years. But the old man had obviously given up the effort.

He gave up and got to his feet to go to his room. On his way out, he stopped and turned round. "Can't you put off going back?" he said.

"Why do you ask?"

"I just thought," the old man said with a thin, embarrassed smile, "it would be good if you stayed on until Diwali. Keshi would be home then."

Nindi kept quiet, for it was simply not possible for him to prolong his stay.

He returned to the terrace. The house subsided into silence. The light in the veranda went off, but that in his mother's room was still on.

After a while, Nindi went in to sit on the edge of his bed. A dusty, grimy bundle containing his school textbooks lay in a corner. A Juan Gris print he had sent Keshi from Leipzig hung on a wall. Keshi had sundry interests, such as old paintings, gramophone records, first editions of books. It was a hard job shopping for Keshi. Nindi himself had no fascination for these things. Even now as he sat idle, he couldn't bring himself to browse through any of the books.

Mother brought him a glass of milk, her last chore

before turning in, and afterwards stood about uncertainly. It was obvious she had something on her mind.

"Why don't you sit down, Mother?"

"I'm in a hurry. I still have to clean up for the night," she said lamely. "Did you go to see Aruna?"

"No, I couldn't."

"You should have. She often asks after you."

"All right – I will," he said to please her.

It was apparent to her he had no intention of keeping his promise. She changed the topic. "Go over to Keshi's for a change. It will do you good."

"I'm fine – don't worry. I should be on my way back to Vienna before long."

"Ah yes! I almost forgot." He was startled at the sudden change in her tone. He looked into her face closely, but it didn't give away anything.

She started across the room but paused short of the door. "Neeta will be here on Sunday. You'll be home for the day, I hope?" she said.

"Sure. I'm looking forward to seeing her."

After his mother had left, he went over to the window. The sultry August night stretched away on all sides. His troubled eyes flitted from the plants in the courtyard to the shadows across the deserted lane. What was he so afraid of? he asked himself. He would be gone in a few days and no one would be any the wiser. Neither his mother nor Aruna, nor anyone else, would have found out he had a girl tucked away in Vienna. Perhaps he should have told them about her long before; it would have made things a lot easier all around. Perhaps, though, his not having told them about her made little difference. He would soon be gone with his secret. Afterwards, it wouldn't matter even if they came to know of it. Not in the long run, anyway. Nothing ever did, especially if one's parents were so very old, he thought wearily.

For once, he was glad Keshi wasn't home. He would have smelled a rat at once. Still, Keshi probably wouldn't have cornered him, but a wall would have come up between them.

A breeze shuffled up the lane. He turned away from the window to go to bed. He put out the light. Lying in bed, he reminisced about his childhood. A quiet boy, Keshi was nicknamed the Chinese mandarin. Neeta and he used to make fun of the youngster behind his back but were awed in his presence. He recalled an incident from the far past and chuckled to himself in the darkness.

When they were very small they used to live at a hill station. One day during their summer vacation, Keshi, Neeta and he wandered over to an overgrown garden behind the cottage. As children, they believed that treasures were buried in abandoned ground. They chose a spot and started digging. They dug for quite some time. Neeta was bored and wanted to give up. Just then the spade struck something hard. It was a big stone. Together, they pushed it aside. With pounding hearts, they looked in the pit beneath it – and stood back aghast.

In the pit lay a twig, a long bleached bone, and a piece of broken glass.

Cautiously they touched their fingertips to each of the things in the pit, one after the other. All of a sudden Neeta started crying and ran away towards the house. The brothers followed her quietly, leaving their find in its place.

That night as they lay in their beds Keshi had asked him, his eyes riveted on a spot in the ceiling directly above him: "Can you tell why Neeta started crying suddenly?"

"She took fright, obviously."

"It was we who were frightened. She wasn't; she is much too sensitive to be afraid."

Nindi looked resignedly at Keshi, whose gaze was still fastened to the ceiling. "Well?"

"When you laid your fingers on those things in the pit, didn't you feel that they were resisting your touch?" Keshi was lost in his thoughts. When he spoke again, it was in a low distant voice: "It's a great thing to be able to resist." He took a deep breath and turned away on his side.

Keshi was the limit, really!

Tonight Nindi couldn't get to sleep for a long, long time. His thoughts turned to the apartment in Vienna where he had spent the last three years of his life. It overlooked a canal off the Danube. The trees along the avenues must have started shedding their leaves, he told himself... He heard his father cough in his bedroom below. He heard him pour water from a gurgling carafe into a tumbler. He heard his mother, so light of foot, go up the passage to put the chain on the front door for the night and retrace her steps to her room. He heard the silence heave with the wind, which filled the curtain over the window even as a shadow swung across the Juan Gris still life on the wall.

On Sunday Nindi went to the swimming pool in the morning. He came back well past midday to find Neeta already home. Her daughter Bulu was with her.

"Guess what I brought for you!" He inhaled deeply of the smell of Bulu's hair, which reminded him of

Neeta's. "I've put away your things in the cupboard."

"But Uncle, you promised to show me how to do a Charleston." Bulu looked up with the eager shining eyes of a child.

"I will, provided you won't ever let anyone else but me dance with you."

"Not even when I'm grown up?" she asked in mock disappointment.

"Of course! As yet you're a mere chit of a girl – a nothing!" When Bulu grew up, he imagined, she would look like a real nineteenth-century Russian princess, just as fragile and beautiful.

They sat over tea in Keshi's room. For Bulu, chocolate was stirred into a cup. Neeta pulled up an easy chair for Father and he lay back in it. In spite of their age, both Neeta and Nindi felt constrained in the presence of their father. Keshi was the only one in the family who could strike up an easy conversation.

"We expected you to visit us. Your brother-in-law was asking after you," Neeta said to Nindi. "What was it kept you so busy?"

"Just busy-ness," he laughed it away. "I go to the swimming pool sometimes and to the club afterwards with Mahip, and so on." He saw a surprised look on Neeta's face and added quickly," I learned to swim over there. You should too. Most girls abroad do."

"At my age? Are you out of your mind?" She laughed aloud, darting a glance at her father. His eyes were closed.

"What's wrong with your age. You're still young." To him, Neeta looked, especially when she laughed, too young to be Bulu's mother; the two of them looked like sisters at least. The passage of time seemed to have left her untouched; like a book kept perfectly clean inside an only slightly soiled jacket.

The afternoon wore on. Bulu meanwhile slipped away to the terrace.

"You should have gone out someplace, Father," Neeta said. "For a man your age, summer in Delhi can be pretty dull and tiring."

"Perhaps you're right. Keshi wrote to us to spend some time with him," he said leaning forward in his chair. "But we didn't dare go alone. We're too old." He laughed with a self-deprecating air.

"Should I write him to come? Then he could escort you."

The old man stared blankly ahead. Then he spoke slowly: "Later, maybe. After *he* is gone."

Neeta looked Nindi in the face. He turned to look out the window. He reached into his trousers pocket for a cigarette, but his hesitant fingers stopped short. He had never smoked in his father's presence; it was not good manners.

Stray sun-rays glimmered off the teacups on the table. A sparrow flew in through the ventilator and fluttered above their heads trapped within the four walls... Nindi realised, quite forcefully and for the first time that summer, how alone and lonely his father was...

Bulu barged in, breaking the tension in the room.

"Well, Uncle, where are my things?" she demanded imperiously.

"What things?" Neeta interposed.

Nindi went over to the cupboard and took out a leather bag, bought in Vienna, from the bottom drawer. The girl could hardly contain herself; with youthful impatience she shot out her hand for the bag. She took it to the tea table, unzipped it and turned it upside down. A large collection of coins fell clinking on to the tabletop. Bulu gazed at the shining pile in disbelief.

"Are these all for me?" she chimed. Rather than a question, it was an exclamation of joy at the certainty that all these coins really belonged to her.

He pulled his chair close to the table and launched into a commentary on the coins – the Austrian shilling, Italian lira, krone of the Faeroe Islands, and so on. He had set aside for her coins of all the countries he had visited. His hand lingered momentarily over a German mark as the memory of the lonely night he had spent on the streets of Berlin returned to him. The rest of the coins, however, evoked no particular emotion.

"Did you go to the Faeroe Islands also?" Neeta asked in surprise.

"You didn't mention that in your letters."

"I only stayed there overnight on my way to Iceland."

"Are those islands as small as they appear on a map?" Bulu asked, carried away by her curiosity.

He pressed his cheek to her palm. "They are each smaller than your palm, my dear."

Bulu was excited.

"Come on, Uncle, show me how to dance a Charleston." She came up close against him.

He looked at Neeta, who had moved her chair back into a corner. Father had already left. She shifted the tea table out of the way. Bulu hurriedly gathered up the coins, even as a wisp of her hair escaped over her shoulder, scattering the brittle late afternoon sun.

Years later he would recall this August evening in his father's house. Bulu was quick to learn; she had no difficulty in following the steps. Fiddling with the knobs of the radio, they had at last succeeded in coaxing from it some kind of dance music, albeit fitful. It was perhaps never meant to accompany a Charleston, but it would have to do. As Bulu whirled about and kicked her legs and looked up at him, he was carried away. They danced closer and more briskly. Bulu came into his arms, her lips parted in a beatific smile, so strikingly like what he had seen during his early days in Vienna on the lips of girls as young as Bulu as they sketched the heady steps of a Charleston for the first time.

"Faster, Uncle!" Bulu whispered in his ear, her eyes bright in her flushed face. Nindi was both surprised at and frightened by her intensity.

"That's enough! Come now," Neeta said from the semi-darkness of her corner.

"Oh no! Not yet." Bulu cried.

Nindi wiped sweat off his forehead. "Let's call it a day, Bulu," he said gently. "Another time, perhaps."

"But when?" Tears of disappointment filled her eyes. "You'll be gone before I've learned the steps well enough." Perhaps she was ashamed of her tears, for she laughed suddenly, and said: "You remember the time you gave me waltz lessons, do you?"

He looked into her eyes and said on impulse, "Come, Bulu, let's waltz."

Bulu looked to her mother with a pleading smile on her lips. She had what perhaps was not, in Keshi's terms, deep feeling, but her irresistible fascination for the waltz puzzled him and somewhat disturbed him. However, he was happy at the moment. Neeta leaned forward in her seat and watched them indulgently. Both Bulu and he tried to drag her to the middle of the floor but she excused herself. The sun set as they danced on and on. The radio crackled the same outdated tune, its notes flickering like a match-flame in a draft. In the dusk, with her head on his shoulder, the tall Bulu appeared to him older than her years: on her breath still lingered the sweetness of a child. Her hair gave off a smell reminiscent of Neeta's, or of his mother's, of a carefree summer at a hill station not so very long ago when he was himself a child.

They pulled away. The spasmodic tune from the radio had finally stopped. Neeta rose to turn on the lights.

"That was quite a dance. You really looked like a master," Neeta laughed in appreciation as he pulled up the chair in which his father had sat earlier in the afternoon and dropped into it to recover his breath. He lit a cigarette.

"Do you go out dancing every evening over there, Uncle?" Bulu asked enviously, gathering her hair at the nape of her neck.

He merely smiled at her.

An exhausted Bulu stretched out on the divan. Neeta went away to help her mother in the kitchen. Nindi waited for a while for Neeta to return. Sleep lay heavily on Bulu's eyelids, but her cheeks were still aflame. Gently Nindi removed her shoes and put them away in a corner.

"Uncle!" the girl called out, opening her eyes.

"Yes, what is it, Bulu?"

"Are you really going away?"

"I'm not going anywhere."

Bulu closed her eyes and turned on her side towards the wall. He put out the overhead light but left the table lamp on before walking quietly out of the room.

He found no one on the terrace. The night was windless and close. Faint moonlight lay in grubby tatters along the huddled rooftops. Opposite him, across the lane, rain-water drains divided the off-white walls into cinema screens on which shapeless shadows appeared now and then.

Before long he retreated to his room, turned on the light and opened his suitcase. Some books on architecture lay on top of his clothes. He reached under these and took out the bottle of cognac discreetly wrapped in a bath towel. He would rather have a drink before anyone came upstairs looking for him; he sorely needed one.

Actually he didn't like to drink, much less drink alone. Not in his father's house anyway, nor brandy. It was only when he couldn't get to sleep that he helped himself to a night-cap. Even as he sipped, all his gnawing fears and thoughts of Vienna fell away, and a sense of well-being and comfort took hold. He would then be ready to let himself sink into sleep.

But tonight, after those dances with Bulu, he was exhausted and knew that getting to sleep would not be a problem. Curiously, however, when he was assured of sleep he would want to keep it at bay: he would rather slip into it of his own free will, as into the depths of the swimming pool.

He poured the brandy. At the same time, a shadow fell on the wall in front of him. it stayed his hand momentarily, but he was in no apparent hurry to turn around: he took a long swill from his glass and felt instantly better.

Then he turned around and saw Neeta in the doorway.

"I wondered if you'd turned in," she said. She came

in and sat down at the foot of his bed. Meanwhile, he managed to push the bottle out of sight under the bed. For a moment he hoped she would leave him alone; he wouldn't have been sorry to see her go.

"Is Bulu asleep?"

"Yes," Neeta said. "She is pretty excitable. You shouldn't have let her dance so long."

"It's all right. She takes after you."

"Surely you could have taken the time to visit us at least once. Your brother-in-law would have been so glad."

There was something in her voice, not an outright sense of injury, but something intangible and elusive which cast a shadow between them.

"You don't mind, do you?"

"I don't," Neeta said, apparently embarrassed. "But do you drink every night?"

"No, not every night. Just once in a while." He reached for the bottle of brandy under his bed.

"Nindi," she began haltingly. He looked at her. Her eyes were intent like Bulu's.

"Yes, Neeta, what is it?"

She continued to stare into his face for a long moment.

"You've changed," she let out slowly, uncertainly.

"You really think so?" he said playfully.

"Don't you?"

"Maybe. I wouldn't know."

They were silent until he queried, "You drop in here often?"

Neeta looked startled. "Not often – only occasionally," she said. "Not quite as often anyway as I did when Keshi was here."

They began to talk about Keshi. His collection of

first editions, photo albums, and prints of old paintings still lay on the top shelf and in the drawers of the cupboard in his room.

Nindi tipped more cognac into his glass. A warmth had begun to spread through his body.

"Look, I've something to say to you." Neeta's distant strained voice broke through the silence. "That's why I followed you up here." He stopped playing with the glass in his hands. He became all attention. He had been waiting for this inevitable moment.

"Can't you stay?" Neeta's voice was flat.

"What good will come of it?"

"Mother and Father are all alone in the house. I wasn't worried when Keshi was around."

"I can't see how my staying on will make a difference: everything here would go on much the same."

"Perhaps you don't even want to stay."

He felt too lightheaded to care any more. "All right, I don't."

Their eyes met, and they held each other's gaze.

"Perhaps what Keshi said is true," Neeta said drily.

"What did he say?"

"That you don't live there alone."

He continued looking into her eyes and said, "Yes, it's true."

"So you're married?"

"No. We only live together."

"What about Aruna? Does she know?"

He drained his glass in a long draught and set it on the floor. "No use telling her, I suppose."

They relapsed into silence. Both had run out of talk. He had an impulse to share with his sister all that had happened to him during the three years away from home, but he held his tongue. It wouldn't make any difference one way or the other, he told himself.

"I think I must be going," Neeta got to her feet. Then she noticed the new paint on the walls. "Did you paint these walls yourself?" She was obviously taken aback.

"How do you like it?" He laughed, and added in the same breath, "I've done the outer walls as well."

"Keshi has a big surprise in store for him."

They walked together slowly across the room to the bookshelves built by Neeta and Keshi long ago.

"Your books are still here," he said to Neeta. He thought it rather strange that Neeta should have left her books behind after her marriage.

Neeta was going over the titles absent-mindedly when she looked around at him suddenly. "Did you ever go to Zweig's Bookshop in Vienna?"

"Come on! How do you suppose one is going to find time for all that?" He had never been interested in books or writers.

"Nindi," she said softly, turning away from the shelves to face him, "don't you feel strange that we're home tonight, together after a long time, but that Keshi is not with us?"

Her words were so charged that he turned away. They stood perilously close to the edge of a territory that their divergent paths had left uncharted between them – an unknown stretch they dared not tread upon together. It had better be left alone.

Each was alone on either side of that territory.

Come September, the trees started shedding their withered, discoloured leaves beneath an open azure sky. The air was crisp and dry, bright and transparent. The city which had seemingly shrunk under the summer sun began to bulge at the seams; the streets overflowed again.

But Nindi stayed indoors most of the time. His mother hardly ever disturbed him; his father kept mostly to himself; and only once, in all those September days did he visit Neeta.

All the time Nindi was home he worried lest his father should think he was bored. So every evening, he changed into fresh clothes and went out, so that his father would believe he was having a good time with friends. All Nindi did, though, was buy cigarettes along the way and kill time at a restaurant until he was sure his father had gone out for his walk. Then he slipped back into his rooftop room.

The day before he was scheduled to leave, he went to the swimming pool once more. He went early, long before Mahip was expected to turn up at the club. It was early September, the air was light and vibrant, and the heat's bite had been blunted.

That day he swam for hours on end. Under water, he could make out a difference: no longer was the water as dark as in July. As he plunged into the pool its water covered him like a clear roof above which a benign sun shimmered like a candle.

He thought he heard a faint rustling, then a rapping sound somewhere deep in the water – or was it the wind above? It sounded like an axe whacking into a tree again and again in an otherwise silent forest. He came up, and the sound ceased. The sun was going down and his teeth chattered from the cold.

He changed and crossed over to the club terrace. He found Mahip there in a corner. All the other chairs on the terrace were empty.

"What a crazy fool you are!"

"Am I too late?" He pulled a chair close to Mahip's.

"Come on, have a drink. It wouldn't do to die of cold on the eve of your departure. Your lips are quite blue."

Nindi ordered hot tea with a dash of rum. Mahip stayed with beer.

"You see," Nindi laughed. "I heard a strange sound in the pool today."

"So now you've started hearing things, too!"

Nindi ignored the jibe. He could still hear a dull hammering in his temples.

They were alone on the terrace. Downstairs, next to the bar, was the dance floor. Now and then fragments of conversation or laughter floated up to them. Nindi paused when it occurred to him that he would not be here this time tomorrow.

The opening bar of a quadrille rose explosively from the dance floor below. It was so loud that even the glasses on the table between them shook nervously. It had not occurred to Nindi that they still danced the quadrille in these parts.

He felt a warmth flow in his veins as he sipped his tea.

"Did you see Aruna?"

"No, I couldn't make it."

Mahip squinted at him over the rim of his mug. "We thought you were in love with her," he sighed, with a puzzled expression on his face.

Nindi looked up sharply but chose not to answer. Three years ago, he tried to recollect...and it surprised him to realise he had no regrets. He was glad he had not seen Aruna; after all, one couldn't face a person one had loved dearly once but now loved no more. Would Mahip understand? He was more likely to take umbrage, though. Aware of his vulnerability, Nindi felt a sudden stab of loneliness.

"I heard you went hiking last year," he side-tracked.

"Yes, we did," Mahip responded eagerly. He had always been a keen hiker, and Nindi had never been able to work out his singular urge. Hiking for Mahip seemed to be like a fashionable craze. "We went right up to the Rohtang Pass," he added smugly. "Keshi was with us too."

They were interrupted by young couples who came up from the dance hall below talking loudly, soft-drinks in hand. They settled into chairs at the other end of the terrace.

Lights around the pool shone in the darkness across the lawn.

"What are you thinking about?"

Nindi shrugged his shoulders and laughed.

"Look," Mahip said, laughing too, "we – all of us – got the impression that you were going to marry Aruna."

Nindi looked up wearily at Mahip. Perhaps Mahip was already a little high, he thought. Had he been drinking by himself before Nindi joined him on the terrace?

The endless evening sky, combed by a searchlight, stretched mutely beyond the darkness above the glow of the city lights. This was where he had grown up, Nindi reminded himself, and it was his duty to stay: everybody who is anybody is sooner or later concerned about his roots; he comes to recognise his debt to the soil on which his feet are planted, where he was brought up, which alone could be his. But he had never given it more than a passing thought – unlike Keshi, who had chosen to enlist in the army.

From the dance hall a very old tune, *The Blue Danube*, carried upwards into the still air. The young couples disappeared quickly down the stairway.

"You must have seen the Danube. Is it really blue?" Mahip inquired.

Nindi smiled to himself as he recalled his early days in Vienna. Blue is a sad colour, he thought wistfully; a spell of melancholy is called blues; there is the black American music... Anyway, it was not the colour in itself but what you made of it that mattered.

"It must be such fun living there," Mahip beamed at him over his umpteenth beer.

"So it is," he agreed. "Look, you must come over someday. I've two sofabeds in the living room. Both Keshi and you would be comfortable." He was feeling nicely warm after another couple of grogs. He told Mahip about the Ringstrasse, about *bierkellers* that could accommodate five hundred clients at a time, and about the large Staat Park, where he used to go on Sundays.

"The trees in the park shed their leaves these days. An orchestra plays every evening, and you can send in your requests, and after they have played your number the conductor bows in your direction."

Then he noticed that Mahip's eyes were hazy with sleep and stupefaction.

"Let's make a move."

"You can come along to my room. I've some port left over," Mahip offered with a yawn.

"I don't think I can. I've yet to pack."

They walked out into the September night. Stars shone in the cloudless sky like polished brass buttons.

They hailed a taxi.

"What time did you say your flight is?"

"Very early. You'll be in bed."

"I'll try to make it," Mahip said, getting into the taxi. He let his head roll on to the back of the seat and immediately passed out.

That night, his last in Delhi, Nindi reached home very late. His mother undid the chain on the front door and stood to one side to let him in. He hurried past her and went whistling up the stairs as if he had no care in the world.

He went straight into the bathroom to rinse his mouth, but the smell of rum still clung to him. He was afraid his mother would notice it. He felt a little giddy. He was pleased he would still be giddy when he hit the bed.

At last he was in his own room. His mother had already gathered his things in a neat pile by his suitcase. His socks and handkerchiefs had been washed, dried and folded. He had nothing much to pack, anyway. Over the last few days he had made some purchases, which included a warm muffler, a pair of shoes, gloves, and two detective novels to read during the flight.

Presently, his mother came in with a label bearing his name and destination in longhand. The largish letters had been formed in ink with a margosa twig, which otherwise is used for brushing the teeth.

"Your father wrote this label for you," she said. "Stick it on your suitcase."

"He needn't have bothered."

"You have the air ticket with you?"

"It's in my pocket."

He began to pack his suitcase.

"Does Neeta know?"

"I told her."

Later, his mother waited on him as he ate. He was not hungry, but he sat over his meal a long time.

"Can't you stop by at Keshi's for a day?"

"I'll try." Of course, it was impossible, but there was no way he could have gotten it across to her.

His mother did not press her point. There was something unusual in the way she sat so quietly. He looked up to see she had turned her face sideways to the wall. He looked closely at her and realised with a twinge how age had shrivelled her.

He started as his mother resumed slowly, "Would you mind terribly if I asked you...to..."

He stared at her.

"...to write to Aruna once in a while," she managed to say at last. "She does care, you know."

At once a wave of impotent anger welled up in him. He said nothing; he wasn't sure whom he was angry with. But his anger subsided quite as suddenly. He was reassured by the thought that his mother did not suspect anything yet.

He made his way to the terrace. The moonlight lay across it as yesterday, ever so dull and feeble. The margosa tree by the wall moved as a breeze picked up.

Back in his room, he wrapped in a bundle the prints of old paintings and the discs he had brought from Vienna for Keshi and put it away in a corner. The Gris still-life remained on the wall. All Keshi's and Neeta's things lay in their accustomed places, as if the two of them had just gone out for a walk. He left the things alone, somehow afraid to touch them.

He turned off the light and lay down on his bed. He

tried to recollect all the summers he had spent with his parents in this house and the others at various times in the distant past, but his mind wandered among trivia. His thoughts turned to the cities of Europe he had visited last summer and the summer before.

His ears caught a faint rustling sound. At first he thought he was hearing it in his sleep, but the next moment he sat up on his bed staring into the darkness. Instantly, his eyes fixed on a moving form clad in white.

"Is it you, Father?"

"Put on the light, will you? I can't see anything."

Nindi was so shaken he at first couldn't find the bedside switch. "What are you doing here?" He was angry in spite of himself.

"I thought you might still be up," his father said defensively.

Nindi did not quite believe him; he had a feeling he had been in the room for quite some time.

"Won't you sit down?" Nindi made to get up from the bed, still annoyed.

"It's all right – I'll just take a minute," his father said.

"Here, have a look at this. Do you like it?"

He looked past his father at the coat draped over the armrest of a chair behind him.

"Try it on," his father said. "Keep it if it fits you. I've no further use for it."

"I already have one."

"You can always use another. After all, you're going to stay there another three years," the old man insisted. "You won't find an overcoat of this quality these days. It keeps out the rain as well."

"But there's hardly any space in my suitcase," he said rather uncertainly.

"Just throw it over your arm. Air passengers carry all sorts of things in their hands."

He kept quiet. His annoyance had given way to a feeling of dreary emptiness.

"Come, try it on."

"It's all right. I'll take it."

The old man looked away. His eyes wandered throughout the room, except in the direction of the overcoat; he seemed to be avoiding it as a criminal avoids the scene of his crime.

After his father had gone, Nindi felt a twitch of regret. Father would have been pleased, he told himself, if he had tried on the coat in his presence.

He lay down on his bed, afraid to turn off the light. It occurred to him that had he not woken, his father would have quietly left the coat on the chair: he still fought shy of giving Nindi anything in person. He remembered how, when he was a schoolboy, his father would leave his pocket money on the desk instead of handing it to him.

He turned on his side. He listened to the sounds of the house. He heard his mother go down the passage and secure the chain on the front door. He heard his father cough in his room now and then.

Somewhere a radio was still playing. A vagrant wind picked up snatches of a song to drop them indifferently on other rooftops.

At last, it was quiet. He turned off the light, and saw the moon crawl slowly in over the threshold.

He tried to get to sleep again... He was skiing with Keshi on the slope at Kufri. There was snow all around. He was flying down when his skis nosed up into something hard. Out of curiosity, he started digging at the place with the upturned end of a ski. Loosened chunks of snow flew around until, abruptly, he stopped. Down there was a pit, and he thought he heard someone crying in it. He peered into it but saw no one there. There was nothing there – except an ashen bone, a sodden branch of a tree, and a piece of broken glass.

He woke up with a start. The house was utterly silent, and he was alone with a splinter of moonlight on his bed.

The Morning Walk

He took his walking-stick and stepped out right foot forward, down the stairs. He believed that if he began the day by putting his right foot foremost, he was less likely to run into trouble. In the morning he got out of bed by rolling over to his right. If his left eyelid twitched, it reminded him of his son who had settled abroad years ago.

Swinging his stick, he set out towards the *nullah*. In fact, the *nullah* could no longer be seen: it had been covered over three years ago by the municipality. But the residents of the district still called his house "the *nullahwalla* house". His friends still wrote to him at the address: Col. Nihalchandra, Nullahwalla House; and the postman never made a mistake in delivering these letters to him.

He kept on walking until he reached a culvert, its whitewashed parapets gleaming in the sun. He stopped here; this was the first stop on his morning walk. He leant his stick against the parapet and hung his shoulder-bag from its crook. Then he stood stiffly erect, as if at attention. He took a breath; he inhaled the air deep into his lungs, gathered it into a tight little blast and blew it out. After a pause, he took another breath, his muscles tensing to control the rush of air... Did he derive some relief from the act?

Nobody knew; he never asked any questions of himself, nor was there anyone else who could have asked him any.

To all appearances, he was not bothered about the schoolboys who had stopped below the culvert and, amazed, were staring up at him – at his tall spare frame, sucking the air deep into himself, shaking like a reed.

"Colonel Sa'b! Colonel Sa'b!"

"Where's your gun?"

"An' where's your sword?"

The boys jeered, screamed, scattered. Their feet splashed in the rain-water as they ran away.

The grass rustled in the wind.

The children's voices buzzed in Nihalchandra's ears, but before long it was quiet again. He filled his lungs one last time with air which eventually surged from his nostrils in a misty gush. He picked up his walking-stick and cleaned its crook with a handkerchief before blowing his nose and wiping his eyes. He slung his bag over his shoulder. His throat pricked from dryness. He could just make out that there was an uneasiness in him, a vague discomfort which he dared not identify yet as thirst. He lived in a fog in which all discomforts remain anonymous. To try to identify and define any one of them would have taken the lid off the Pandora's box – and that was dangerous. No, he was better off with the fog that blurred alike all definitions and the need to define.

Further ahead, beyond the culvert, was a large stretch of level ground. A part of it was being used as a washing-place by the *dhobis* and the rest was clad with trees. The *nullah*, hidden in the town, flowed breezily out here in the open. The sun glancing off the flat-topped stones along its edges was agonisingly bright. Nihalchandra took out his sun-glasses from the bag, put them on and looked across the open space. He saw a pool of soft muted light – a cool shade of darkness. He stepped into it and began to pick his way slowly among the stones.

The washerwomen beating clothes on the smooth stones looked up, their hands in mid-air, as Nihalchandra passed by, picking his way with single-minded concentration, slowly and soundlessly. Some dogs snooping about at the *ghat* were provoked at the sight of him; they growled and broke into a run after him but pulled up just out of reach of his walking-stick. Nihalchandra went on unconcerned. To him the barking dogs and the squealing children were just part of the wayside scene: perceived through a film of smoke, heard through a noise of droning...

The spell broke where the forest began. Here there was no sound, nor sunshine except where it lay bunched in tremulous spangles under the trees. Nihalchandra had no more use for the sun-glasses. He shifted his bag to the other shoulder. He loosened his coat buttons and the November wind, turning swiftly, chilled him. The tall trees, the low bushes, and among them the flaming silk-cotton blossoms, and the whistling wind – these reminded Nihalchandra of the forests near Gwalior where, a long time ago, he had often gone hunting with his army friends. But he no longer remembered it clearly. Sometimes, however, a picture flashed in his mind and he saw a part of his past surface for air before diving back into the depths... And Nihalchandra plunged headlong into a thicket and disappeared.

It would be some time before he could locate where

he was. He gave himself away as the undergrowth crackled and swished, as if an animal were fleeing, and then his head appeared suddenly between the bushes: here, then gone. Anyone chancing upon him would have been astonished to see how fast he ran at his age, with walking-stick and shoulder-bag to boot. But for Nihalchandra it was a routine exercise. Indeed, more than an exercise, it was his way of meditating. He had a rapt look about him, giving rise to the illusion that he was standing still, as though his long spindly legs were working under him by themselves...until by and by his legs too came to a standstill, leaving his aged heart alone to thump against his ribs. He opened his half-closed eyes, and looked about him.

There, right in front of him, stood the Hawa Mahal – a Moghul monument of yellow sandstone, basking in the November sun.

Sweat ran in runnels from Nihalchandra's white hair down along his temples. He shook his head, mopped his brow with his handkerchief, and rested his walking-stick and the bag against one of the steps leading to the Hawa Mahal. He panted. Fatigue oozed from his body as from the old ruins.

This was his second stop of the morning.

This Hawa Mahal must have been a halting-place at one time for the Moghul army contingents from Delhi. Or, could it be that the Emperor himself would come here occasionally to picnic? Yes, this might just explain its elaborate architecture and secluded location. Nihalchandra had come upon this treasure fortuitously. He had wandered from the course of his morning walk in the forest when his eyes fell upon the building; it just seemed to materialise out of thin air.

It had white marble steps, balconies with ornamental lattice-work screens, large round ventilators, and – what fascinated him most – a blue dome sparkling like a cool, polished gem. This blue, set against the grey, pale tones of the forest, was particularly pleasing.

Nihalchandra sighed deeply, but the breath came out as a groan that trailed off somewhere between "Aah!" and "O Lord!" He took his khaki raincoat from the bag and spread it out along the bottom step. This was his favourite spot. From here he had not only a choice view of the dome looming above the balconies but also a chunk of the November sun. What more need he ask for?

Nothing.

Nothing stirred. No sounds, no movement – but for the wild screeches of a hungry bird tearing through the air above him which prodded his own hunger, and he reached into his bag for his lunch packet.

A boiled egg, tomato and cucumber sandwiches, hot coffee in a thermos – Devi Singh the housekeeper had packed his bag neatly and carefully, as if he were journeying to the other end of the world. The simple fellow had overlooked nothing; he had not even forgotten to put in packets of salt and black pepper. A transistor radio his son Mannu had brought for him from abroad to fill the void of his dull days nestled in another corner. Many a time he had thought of giving it to Devi Singh: poor chap, he was left alone in the house all day long; he could certainly do with a little recreation, he told himself. But somehow he couldn't part with it. The dumb radio spoke to him in his son's voice: "You have practically nothing to do the whole day. Why don't you listen to the radio once in a while?" At such moment, a dreary silence closed about him; he stretched out yawning and mumbled: "Ah Lord! Where's the time for all this? I don't have even a moment to myself."

Who was Nihalchandra talking to? To his son, who was abroad; to his wife who was in the next world; or to his Lord, who was nowhere? Perhaps even he did not know. The wind already bore many voices, it bore away his too. Had someone asked him, since he said he had not a moment to himself, what it was that he actually did, he would have immediately retorted, "Why, don't you see I'm eating!" or some such. And that would have been true, too, at the moment. Eating, seeing, walking, sleeping – these were among the activities consequent upon life and had to go on...and in the meantime, he went on talking to himself and listening to his own voice.

Listening. That Nihalchandra did even while asleep. His eyes drooped with sleep as soon as he had finished eating. He gathered the bread crusts and broken egg shells on a scrap of newspaper and put it to one side. He rolled his bag into a pillow, placed it at one end of the raincoat spread on the ground, and lay down, stretching out fully, legs apart. But before he could go to sleep, birds descended on the leftovers; they pecked at the food vigorously, frequently tearing holes in the paper beneath...and to Nihalchandra it seemed that it was his sleep rather than the paper that was being torn apart. Soon the kites swooped down, scaring away the other birds; they grabbed beakfuls of the remnants and rose on flapping wings while others dived overhead...dropping through layers of sleep and scattering his dreams. In the shifting shadows cast by low clouds, the blue dome seemed to tilt. Nihalchandra seemed to be looking at himself through a swaying curtain: he saw a man lying flat on his back, a rolled-up bag for a pillow, a raincoat fluttering in the wind. He waited with a pounding heart: she might be here any moment. She would come but stand a little apart, a skipping rope dangling playfully from her neck.

"Nihali! O Nihali!

Your pockets are empty.

Alas, Nihali!

Are they all empty?"

As the voice drew steadily closer, Nihalchandra lay still, absolutely stock-still, holding his breath, his throbbing heart concealed under his hands. He was afraid that if she caught even a hint of movement, she would flee at once and her voice would be lost in the chatter of trees. Basically, it was a question of faith – she had to make sure that no risk was involved, and so she advanced slowly, step by watchful step, all alert, not because she did not trust Nihalchandra, but simply because he was alive and, his apparent harmlessness notwithstanding, could be dangerous. She therefore kept at arm's length, but one of her hands reached out to his regulation overcoat to search its oversized pockets one after the other; her fingers moved gently, almost caressing their linings: "Nihali, O Nihali!"

What did she want with him? What mysterious motif were her fingers drawing in his empty pockets? Her touch set him on fire, and sent his blood pulsing like a maddened bull, out of breath, crashing through fences, dragging behind it his heart enclosed in his time-worn bones...and Nihalchandra gave in: he let the skeletal iron-barred door of his body fly open to allow the captive to escape. *Let go*, a voice within him said, *how long can you hold back?*

No leaf stirred. It was an hour of peace and quiet. The afternoon shadows crawled up the ruins of the Hawa Mahal. Nihalchandra lay with bated breath, stiffening at the slightest crackle of the grass. He shut his eyes tight as the sun broke into iridescent rings under his eyelids...and soon he floated away, leaving his body behind, to proceed towards his third, and last, stop of the day.

Here at his last destination he was invisible and so no longer apprehensive or afraid of witnesses. His body lay prone in the shadows of the Moghul monument. She crept up to him, pulled her *chunni* low between her breasts, threw its ends over her shoulders, and sat down huddled beside him – then Nihalchandra sensed that the iridescent rings behind his eyelids were in fact the glowing dots of her *salwar-kameez*, so near that he could have easily touched them. But he resisted the temptation, pretending that he was seeing nothing, and let her fingers play upon his body.

"O Nihali, are they really all empty?"

No, they were not all empty; today he had brought everything. Would she care to see? *Com'on, let me show you.* He raised his head just a little, and her dark grieving eyes, which could see through his betrayals in a moment, consumed him.

And what did the old fogey have to show to her anyway? A rotten plum, a dead partridge, the carcass of a cricket, cat's whiskers, or candyfloss? These were the things he used to stuff into his pockets for her when she was a small girl.

There was nothing in his pockets today that was familiar to her. There were just so many papers; a bank book, letters old and recent, a property deed and, among them, a blue booklet. She started at this last. It was Col. Nihalchandra's passport, which he always carried with him so that in case of emergency the police could get his address. He took care to go to the passport office every third year for its renewal; it would come in handy, he thought, if ever he decided to visit his son. *You haven't yet overcome your longing, Nihali?*

Longing was a word that fluttered about him like a moth. Indeed, was there any such thing as longing any more, in whose shadow he could have settled down to rest, his wings tucked under him? He peered into himself and saw a girl where the longing should have been. Who was this girl? Pale, round-faced, dusty tousled hair, a *chunni* about her neck, a skipping-rope trailing behind her over the last fifty years.

Her head bent, she was gazing intently at a snapshot she had found in his pile of papers. Nihalchandra could not overcome his curiosity. He turned to look down at the photograph while the girl looked up.

"Who is this woman?"

He winced, taken by surprise.

"My wife," he said at last.

"Is that the truth?"

"What do you mean?" He was a little embarrassed. Something heaved inside him.

"What are these mountain ranges?"

"Mountains?" Nihalchandra's attention had wandered. No, this was not a dream. The mountains were right there, bare and gleaming in the sun. He had been posted to Ladakh then. Two Buddhist monks were coming down a flight of stairs from a monastery in the foreground, looking sideways at his wife; but she, seemingly unaware of the camera, was looking in the direction of the shops in the street below.

The face looking out of the photograph was, of course, his wife's. There was no hint yet on it of her terminal illness, nor of the pain that lay ahead. But was she seeing it then? *No, no, Nihalchandra! It's not she, it's you who sees it.* She looked happy, her lips slightly parted; and she was aware of his presence, the mountains behind the monastery, the Buddhist monks on the stairs, the second-hand clothes on rods in front of the shops: a complete moment captured by the camera. How the wind had risen! It blew the loose end of her sari across her face again and again. But, surprisingly, everything lay still in the photograph, calm and peaceful: no trace of the wind at all.

Over there was the girl's finger, soiled, impaling his wife on a smudged piece of paper.

"Nihali," the girl said gently, "do they ever come to see you?"

"Who are you talking about?" he asked timorously.

"Your son?"

"He is abroad."

"And this one here?" The girl looked down at the photograph.

"You are crazy! She is no more."

"And you? What about you?"

"What about me, Katto?" He spoke her name for the first time – and that was out of fear. "What about me? What do you mean?"

Nihalchandra stared at her with his lost, hungry eyes. It struck him that Katto, after all these years, had begun to look like a dwarf – so small and diminutive. Long ago when she was young, she did look taller. Did time flow backwards? No, this was an illusion. In childhood, perhaps everything looks bigger than it actually is – one's house, trees, parents, and... Nihalchandra jumped as the girl turned round to whisper in his ears: "And love, too – isn't it, Nihali?"

He came to with a start. Who was it? Whose the voice? A clumsy cry from somewhere deep within, which rises in the wilderness of age, knocks at the doors. The doors open, but there is nothing beyond. There is nothing in sight. There is neither love nor pain of love; neither pain nor anything else; not even the wife's face or the memory of the son. Absolutely nothing. Only he by himself, all alone. *You, Nihalchandra, who are you?*

Thud...thud...thud. She was skipping rope. Up, down, up again the next moment. Her quick footfalls resounded among the ruins and against his closed eyes.

While Nihalchandra slept, kites came down to perch beside the sparrows on the balconies. They ate his leftovers before turning their avid attention on him, wondering if his body also was a part of their meal. They were disappointed when Nihalchandra opened his eyes... He saw a blue fragment of the November sky break away from his sleep to hang above the intense blue of the dome. "Devi Singh," he called softly. But then he realised he was not at home, that he lay out here in the open. He wanted to wet his throat with a sip of coffee and reached out for the thermos but his hand fell instead on a pile of papers.

A wind riffled his papers – the pension documents, letters, passport, snapshots. Nihalchandra jerked his head in their direction. How was it that they were lying out there? he asked himself. He could not recall taking them out of his pockets. Abashed, Nihalchandra did not dare question the reality of what happened; he simply accepted it. As for his papers, he felt closer to them than to men. They were his pets which had never deceived him. Eyes closed, he had only to touch their ageing familiarity with his fingertips for instant recognition: this is Mannu's letter, this is the bank passbook, this, the Ladakh snapshot, and – and this? His exploring fingers stopped in their tracks. He opened his eyes and saw a postcard Devi Singh had written to him from his village.

The thought of Devi Singh disturbed him. He might be waiting up, hunched on the veranda. How many times must he have warmed his food, or unlatched the front door to look down the street for him. Nihalchandra often returned home late to find a sullen Devi Singh staring quietly at him with his large peasant's eyes reflecting deep concern and curiosity. A silent question would swim across his face: "Where do you go, after all? You go for a morning walk and do not show up till evening. If something were to happen to you, where would I look for you?" Nihalchandra would think up a pretext on the spur of the moment, but deep within him a fear smouldered lest Devi Singh should decide to write to Mannu about him. Before going away, Mannu had warned him: "You'll have nobody except Devi Singh to look after you. If he left, you'd be helpless." Helpless? All right, so what? I'd have my cot on the veranda and no need of anyone around me. Like day, like night: it's all the same to me... His anger overflowed, a helpless, mournful anger, as futile and unproductive as rainwater in the desert.

The desert – that's where I had my last posting,

Nihalchandra reminisced, his hand still on his papers. It was a place on the Indo-Pakistan border in Rajasthan. The desert stretched away on all sides. It was amusing to recall how he had then wanted to settle down there, how he thought he had reached the last station in life. He would go for long walks in the desert and relax on the sand dunes unvisited by memories of his wife or son. In that solitude he had felt he was within reach of some universal truth, that he was beginning to fathom the darkness that had isolated him at the ragged end of his life. It was surprising how the truth that had eluded him in the company of the Buddhist monks in Ladakh should dawn on him in the wind-swept desert... *What truth, Nihali?*

Nihalchandra looked around. Something whirled inside him and strained upwards through his accumulated fatigue, indecisions and the burden of years to fill his throat to the brim – but whatever it was remained unsaid. There was nobody there. The November sun broke on the treetops. The blue dome of the Hawa Mahal rose in the air like a huge clenched fist. Silence. No kites any more, nor sparrows. Not even the thudding sounds of anyone skipping rope. Just the wizened sun turned to stone, insensate, cold, grey.

Nihalchandra sat still a while longer. Then he stood up, pulling himself to his feet as if he were some stranger. He gathered together all his papers, shoulder-bag, the empty lunch packet, thermos flask, walking-stick – everything he had – before leaving. He had overlooked nothing; nothing was left behind as he turned his back.

The road of return was the road he had come by. It ran across uneven rocky ground, winding among trees and undergrowth with, away on either side, anthills splotched yellow and white with bird droppings. Nihalchandra went on unheeding; no thought distracted him. Only stray images skimmed across his mind before disappearing: Devi Singh's face, his own house, the rustle of papers in his pockets – scraps of images and sounds that blew away ahead of him. He seized one, another seized him. The single-minded concentration of the morning, when he was running towards the Hawa Mahal, eyes closed, was long since gone. What remained was the desperation of seeing nothing, eyes open.

Just ahead was a cluster of trees with a large welcome patch of shade. The leaves underfoot made the going somewhat easier, but a bush caught at his coat. He stopped to disengage himself cautiously. He thought he was being followed, that there were soft-soled feet somewhere behind him. He turned around: there was nobody in sight, just the trees, their heads held high, and the low bushes, and the quivering rings of the sun beneath. He had a strange sense of having seen it before. A long, long time ago, alone in his garden at home, a girl used to follow him about unseen. He had wanted to call to her, but a hand had always reached out to throttle him: "Don't," a voice spoke within him. "You have your whole life ahead of you." Ahead, ahead...until he had dragged himself along to this moment.

What life, Nihalchandra?

As if in answer, there was a short rattling sound somewhere in the branches overhead. He looked up. At first he saw nothing. There were two trees leaning towards each other. The blue sky showed through their branches. He could not make out the source of the sound. He supposed it came from a bird on some upper branch, taking off or alighting, but he could see no bird either. All was quiet again.

Nihalchandra started on, but hesitated before something swaying above him. He adjusted his glasses and as he looked again, his gaze held.

He found himself under the immense spread of a giant banyan tree. One of its boughs had swung low, gnarled and coarse and bent like an elbow, from which hung a rope swaying gently, slowly, as if it were a hooded serpent mesmerised by the nasal notes of a pipe. He was surprised to see that the rope had not been tied to the bough; it had merely been thrown over the bough, its ends hanging freely in mid-air. At either end it had a tiny henna-coloured wooden grip, worn away by use, dust and sweat.

Nihalchandra could not take his eyes off the swaying rope. The air was still. The breathless forest seemed no larger than a nest. Nihalchandra stood motionless, head up. He looked more like a jungle creature than a human – a large, old animal stopped in its tracks at an unfamiliar sound. He was so tall that the rope was within easy reach; he could have easily pulled it down, but he made no move. "Listen, are you there?" he whispered tenderly. An animal cry gurgled from his lungs; it beat about desperately to break loose...then he heard it; the cry had finally escaped. Nothing stopped it, no unseen hand stifled it this time. It echoed among the trees and the undergrowth across the forest resounding through the stretch of years from his childhood to old age.

No one answered his cry: there was nobody there. A

wind had risen, the trees were rustling, and the two ends of the rope were swinging drunkenly. He stood expecting her to emerge at any moment from behind a bush to claim her skipping-rope, but she didn't. He waited as time ran out. He heard neither her laughter nor any crackling of branches. There was no sign to convince him or to indicate that she had visited him earlier in the afternoon, or had sat by him and searched his pockets as he slept – except that when he woke, he had found his papers scattered on the ground.

Nihalchandra, did you really wake up?

The wind died down as darkness gathered. Occasionally, though, the forest exhaled a sultry gust that whistled over the treetops, blew across the washing-*ghat* rousing the dogs, traversed the *nullah* and stopped at the outer door of Nihalchandra's house.

A sleepy Devi Singh started time and again on hearing the sounds of the dark night. He had spent his childhood in the hills and was familiar with the speechless longings of the forest that were lent a voice by the soughing trees and animal cries. He pattered over to the front door every so often to look out, but in vain.

He had dozed off in the kitchen. Already he had warmed Nihalchandra's meal twice. Often Nihalchandra did not return home from his morning walk until after midday, but rarely did he stay out till after dark. On such days, he would slip in stealthily and go straight to bed. But the beat of his walking-stick on the stairs would give him away to a miffed Devi Singh, who remained in the kitchen on purpose. Before long Devi Singh's heart would begin to ache, and he would make tea and bring it over. But Nihalchandra, lying on his bed, eyes closed, pretended he was unaware of his presence.

Tonight the bed was empty. His slippers lay under it on the floor. A washbasin and a jug of hot water, turned quite cold by now, stood in a corner. Devi Singh built a fire to warm up the room so that Nihalchandra could go to bed without having to bother him, right after eating. Devi Singh's eyes grew heavy with sleep. He thought he should go over to the neighbour's to inform him that the Colonel Sahib had not yet returned, but he held back for fear of the police. It was probably better to wait quietly, he told himself. The Colonel should be home shortly: an old man, where could he go alone?

It was a comforting thought. Nihalchandra, indeed, had nowhere to go. He could only come back, every single day of the three hundred and sixty-five, without fail, until the very last day of his life.

Devi Singh sat up on hearing a rattling sound. Was there someone at the door? No, it was the wind. He sat awhile in the dark kitchen, then went into Nihalchandra's bedroom. The fire crackled and snapped. He turned over the split logs with a poker and scraped off the ashes. When the hissing flames licked them again, he stretched out on the floor by the bed.

At last when Devi Singh could stand it no longer, he slipped out of the house and took the road along which Nihalchandra walked every morning – across the *nullah*, the washing-*ghat*, and away beyond the thin stream of clear water.

The moon had climbed above the trees. The forest glowed in the bright moonshine. Then Devi Singh saw him in the distance, waving to him with both hands.

He stopped at once. He was amazed to see that the Colonel, in spite of his familiar clothes and body and face, was looking strangely like a fourteen year old, so fresh and virginal and eager. He heard the Colonel call out to him, beckoning to him with upraised hands. Devi Singh cast off his fear and burst into a run and pulled up quite close to him under the branch from which he was hanging.

Nihalchandra's body was hanging from a noose at the end of a skipping-rope fastened to the bough above. His belongings were scattered on the ground, his pockets turned inside out. Empty. The body swung, the branch swayed and the tiny wooden grips of the rope knocked him on the head.

Deliverance

The schoolteacher was the first person I met in this small, neglected and remote town in the mountains. It was raining as I got down from the bus. In the past three hours I had travelled through three different seasons: sunshine in Bhuvali, clouds over Ramgarh, and here the rain. The driver had pulled up by the roadside in the middle of the town, hurling from the roof-rack the wretched luggage I'd brought all the way from Delhi – an old hold-all that had belonged to my father and an outmoded tin trunk with torn labels from previous journeys still stuck on it like squashed roaches.

I stood there by the roadside, my battered luggage beside me, imbibing the downpour. Rain has a way of stripping man and town of pretension. I clutched my briefcase to my chest, for it seemed, in that desolate place, the only reminder of civilisation and of my own respectability. It also contained the papers that had brought me from my home in the distant metropolis.

By and large, Indian towns are dreary and oppressive. Besides, it was cold, dark and raining. As the bus pulled out, I desperately wanted to jump aboard and request the driver to take me to Bhuvali and Haldvani on the way back to Delhi...to the fold of familiar life, its light and warmth and safety. But the bus did not stop or turn back; it rattled farther up the road. I watched it move off, its tail-lights red clots on the sheet of rain.

I looked about me. There were some shops and cheap eating places across the road and, in the cliff behind them, three or four lantern-lit hollows. In the lowest niche close to the bus shelter was a tea stall with a burlap awning in front, under which sat a few men on benches. I held my briefcase over my head like an umbrella, but my trunk and hold-all were left soaking in the rain and slush, an even more piteous sight than I was.

I looked at the group in the tea-shop, hoping someone would come to my aid. But perhaps I'd remained unnoticed behind the wall of rain. It seemed to have screened me off from the rest of the world. The couple of passengers who had alighted here with me had long since disappeared into the darkness.

Suddenly I saw an umbrella hovering in front of me as though unable to make up its mind whether I was a man of flesh and blood or a ghost. Then a hill man's lean face peeped from under it.

"Is that your luggage?" he asked, pointing to my trunk and hold-all on the ground.

"Yes," I said miserably.

"Where do you have to go?"

"Isn't there a hotel nearby?" I almost whined with helplessness.

"A hotel? In this place?" He looked at me incredulously, as if I longed for heaven without having to die.

"Any place where I could stay?"

"For how long?" A faint curiosity shone in his eyes.

At a loss to answer, I just stared back at him. When

I'd left home I'd not thought in terms of days or
weeks. Before I could say anything, he held out his
umbrella partly over me. Instead of me alone getting
wet, now both of us were getting drenched.

"There's a rest-house some two miles from here.
But the road climbs uphill all the way."

"Can I get a coolie?"

"In this weather?" His eyes took in the row of shops
before settling again on me. He picked up my trunk
by its handle.

"Come with me," he said.

He strode away without waiting for me. It was too
late then to ask for him to stop. I had no option but to
grab my hold-all and follow. I was surprised that a
man so thin could walk so fast with a trunk in one
hand and an umbrella in the other.

The bus stand and the shops receded as we climbed.
It was hard to keep pace with him. I was being
dragged along it seemed, in his wake. Now and then
my shoes got stuck in squelching mud and submerged
pot-holes. He turned once and said something that I
could not catch; I could hear only my heart pounding,
which got worse with each step. Sweat mingled with
rain washed down my face.

When I think of that climb I'm surprised I made it
at all, so soon after a long, tiring journey and despite
gnawing unease. So far, I had advanced only in years,
never before up a mountain; and I've always been the
sort of man whose biological alarm clock begins to
ring midway up a flight of stairs. Besides, for the first
time in my life I had set foot – much against my will –
in a town where I was a complete stranger. Had it
been left to me, I wouldn't have crossed my threshold
to come all the way here. But I had had nothing to say

about it. The choice had been made by the someone whom I had come to seek.

He opened the door. "Here we are," he said.

It was so dark inside I could see nothing. I lingered in the doorway, trying to keep out of the rain. Soon there was a scraping, then a flash from a burning matchstick as he lit a hurricane lamp. Only then did I realise that he had not brought me to a *dharmshala* or a lodge, but to his own place. I hesitated at the door. I'd have stood there undecided a while longer perhaps, had a blast of wind not swept me forward.

Is there any such thing as will? Perhaps it is one of man's fondest illusions. Even as our will strides ahead, we ourselves lag behind, dragged along anyhow. The will goes on, no matter if it cleaves us into several parts. One part of me was left behind at home; another, powerless to move, stood inside the open door, shivering in the rain-soaked draught – while yet another looked on helplessly. The schoolteacher had led me to his room much the same way as the wind had blown me in. I had had no say in the matter.

"Please, sit down," he said, indicating his low-slung tape-bed which, besides a stool, was the only piece of furniture in the room. He pulled up the stool and started to unfasten the laces of his sodden, muddy shoes.

"I asked you to take me to a hotel," I said irritably.

"Come on now! Take this for a hotel room, if it helps any. Tell me, where would you go in this weather?" he said with a laugh.

I wished I could walk out, leaving my things on the floor. His laughter, the mean walls swaying with the lantern flame, my body spattered with mud – did any of this make sense? It had to make sense, of course, or I wouldn't be here, I told myself. I closed the door behind me on wind, rain and darkness, and walked into the room.

At first glance it looked like a hovel, dank and gloomy, suspended in air, open to vagrant clouds which could enter at will, although the fumes and smoke within seemed reluctant to leave. It gave on to what looked like a *godown* where a kerosene stove on a wooden slab and some utensils could be seen: evidently, he cooked his food there. In another corner were a pail of water, a brass mug and a low, slatted seat, which meant it served for bathing also. There was a barred window in a wall strung with his washing hung out to dry under the eaves; the laundry was, of course, now dripping wet.

He was lighting the stove, his back towards me; but he kept an eye on me to make sure I wouldn't give him the slip. I am not a heavy man, but I was sunk so deep in his low cot that my bottom was almost scraping the floor.

He brought tea in glasses and squatted down cross-legged on a mat opposite me.

"This is your first time out here, isn't it?" he said.

"Yes."

"I could tell the moment I saw you."

I looked up into his long, sallow face behind the plume of steam spiralling up from the tea in his hand.

"It wasn't hard to tell," he continued. "When you got down from the bus, you kept standing there by the roadside in the rain. Anyone from this town would have hurried away at once." He laughed again, displaying yellow, but not dirty, teeth – teeth that went well with his pale, weather-beaten face.

"We have very few tourists around this time of the year," he observed after a pause, regarding me with curiosity, as if he expected that at the mention of tourists I'd confide in him right away the reason for my visit in this bad weather. But I kept silent. I had already made a mistake in coming here with him; I did not wish to make another.

"How long have you been living here?" I asked, parrying his implied question.

"Five...no, six years." He placed his glass on the floor and counted on his fingertips. "I came to this place in the year when Shastriji died in Tashkent. I remember hearing the sad news in a hospital bed here."

"You were hospitalised then?" I said, as if offering my sympathy.

"My uncle, who was a doctor at the hospital, brought me over for medical treatment, although there was no dearth of physicians at Almora, where I lived. Anyway, when I was up and about again I learnt the local high school had a vacancy for an English teacher. I got the job." He smiled. "I'd come here for a cure, little knowing it would also solve my problem of unemployment."

"So you don't belong here? This isn't your house?"

"Would you call this shack a house?" His eyes flitted mournfully across the room to the bucket in the corner, the stove on a plank, the wan lantern flame, and back to me buried in the bed: all objects of pity.

"Are you cold? Shall I make a fire?"

"No, please don't bother," I said, "I'm fine." I was fine if fine meant growing numb, so numb indeed that even fatigue fell back in despair. I could only see the things outside – a rainy night, a leaking roof – deep down inside, I felt nothing. He was upset at my aloofness, my lack of response, and probably felt guilty about bringing me along.

"There is a forest rest-house here, you know," he offered helpfully.

"But you have to have official permission to say there, don't you?"

"That's true," he agreed. "But the caretaker isn't so fussy if one wishes to stay only for a day or two... How long will you need to stay there, anyway?"

There was no hint of inquisitiveness in his tone this time. All he wanted was to be of help. His gaze rested on me, steady and even. I could have confided in him then and there. I suspected he had already figured out that I was neither a pilgrim nor a tourist. Who was I? What was I doing here? I was suddenly overcome with despair and weariness. In order that he could make sense of what I had to say, I'd have to go into my family history. But I doubted if he would understand even then the compulsions of my visit. I'm not sure what he saw in my face in the pale half-light. Was it the desperation of middle age, or something else? But whatever it was, he did not persist. He went out to the terrace to collect his dripping clothes and then wrung them out in a corner of the kitchen.

Left to myself, I heaved a sigh of relief. Presently, I rolled out my bedding on the floor. The lantern was kept on a tripod by my head. In its yellow light I took out a sheaf of papers from my briefcase. I wanted to look them over one last time. I was like a student preparing for his examination the next morning who suddenly discovers that his notes are in a mess, devoid of meaning, worthless. The paper of the property deed left by Father was already fusty and brittle with age. The deed itself looked all the more forlorn in the dimly lit room. Among its pages were three letters, one from my elder brother and another from our younger sister, both easily distinguishable by the handwriting. The third was folded and rather crumpled; Mother had sneaked it to me before I left for the bus terminus, and I'd hurriedly thrown it among my papers. Mother pinned each letter of the alphabet carefully down on the sheet of paper quivering under her pen, much like her trembling lips. What could she have written? I still had not read her letter, nor did I want to. In the feeble light the letters of the living appeared as dead as the papers left by the deceased. If I held out the sheaf over the stove, in a moment our house and all the family, the pulls and pressures of relationships among the living and between the living and the dead, would be consumed by the flames... Only I would survive – and he, whom I had come this far to see.

The schoolteacher's shadow fell across the papers in my hand. He was standing at the door to the kitchen, his hands wet, the sleeves of his shirt turned up above the elbows.

"Are you preparing to contest a lawsuit?" He smiled at me.

I returned the papers to the briefcase. He was right, in a way. I had to face the hearing tomorrow – after fully ten years; and I was seized with a maddening desire to seek him out at once and get it over with and catch the morning bus back to Delhi. But the schoolteacher broke in on my vicious thoughts: "You should freshen up. I've heated the water."

I spent the night at the schoolteacher's. I had with

me my own bedding, so that was not a problem; but
he became a little emotional about who should occupy
the cot. He insisted on giving place to me and
sleeping on the floor himself. I didn't have the heart
to tell him that his rocking cot would only ensure me
a night of hallucinations about earthquakes. But I
might yet have to endure one: I was afraid he would
create a scene over the question of meals. My wife
had packed a tiffin to last me a lifetime. I suggested to
him that instead of cooking for the night, we should
do justice to the lunchbox together. Owing to the cold
weather, the food had not spoiled despite the
twelve-hour journey. It was fresh, too, with the
intimacy, concern and care of a distant household.
When he saw the containers full of fried *purees*,
pickle, vegetables and seasoned rice *pulaav*, a wistful
look swept over his face – as if he regretted having
taken pity on one who apparently did not need it.
But he said nothing and left to warm up the food
on the stove.

His room was as untidy as the kitchen was clean.
Books covered with layers of dust and old magazines
lay in a pile on the floor. The ceiling was black with
soot. A discoloured cupboard stood in a niche, its
drawers stuck halfway and his garments hanging over
the edges. On the whole, it looked as untended and
cheerless as a room in a *dharmshala*. It must be
terribly lonely to have to live in it alone all year
round. Maybe he had brought me along because he
was too lonely. I wasn't surprised that he knew
nothing about me; what was surprising was that,
having taken me in, he should choose not to ask me
who I was and where I had come from. I had a
nagging suspicion that perhaps he already knew

everything. That would explain why he had gone to meet the bus in such rain. But who could have told him to expect me – except the one whom I had come to see?

"Dinner is ready," he announced, setting a tray. "Hurry up! It will get cold in a minute.

"Won't you eat also?"

"I eat early in the evening before going out for my walk. It ensures sound sleep...please, go ahead."

He seated himself on a mat opposite me. As I ate, a vague sadness overtook me. My thoughts went to my family. By this time, my wife must have gone downstairs to see Mother, leaving the children in their rooms to do their studying. From this distant, stark place, they appeared like creatures from another planet. It was hard to believe we had all been together until this very morning.

"Look, it has stopped raining. We'll have a clear day tomorrow." He sounded excited, like a child.

My hand stopped short of my mouth as I turned to look out. Little rivulets were still sloshing down outside from the sloping tin roof. There was a thin mist beyond the eaves through which the stars shone as if scrubbed clean.

"Is your school nearby?"

"I forgot to tell you. In fact we are sitting in the outbuilding in the schoolyard."

"Don't tell me!" I looked around me in amazement.

"Well, this room is a part of the school premises. The management let me move in because it had no other accommodation to offer... Anyway, the school is closed at present for winter holidays."

"Don't you go out somewhere during the holidays?"

"I don't really like to. However, I do go down to

Almora once in a while."

"Don't you feel lonely here?"

He was silent for a long moment. Then he said thoughtfully, "In a way, yes. Sometimes. Still I think I'm better off here than at Almora. Besides, if I feel like it, I can always go over to the Baba's."

"Baba – who is he?"

He cast me a searching glance. Then a thin little smile formed on his lips. "There is but one holy man here."

I could no longer restrain myself. "Did he tell you anything about me?"

"About you?" He was obviously baffled.

"About my coming here."

"Why, have you come to see him?" He looked genuinely surprised.

"I hear people come from far-off places to receive his blessings."

"But in this kind of weather?" He stared at me sceptically.

"I'd some leave to spare. I thought this was as good a time as any to visit him... Does he live far away from here?"

He sat brooding a while. "Not very far away," he said rather indifferently. "Maybe about a mile uphill."

It seemed he was annoyed. Perhaps he did not believe me, for one had to be a little crazy to come all the way in this weather to a little-known town tucked away in the mountains to see a holy man hardly known beyond its borders.

Later, he gathered the dirty plates and took them into the corner where he kept the pail of water. For long afterwards the only sounds that filled the room were a pernickety clatter and clang of the plates and the splash-and-slurp of the water.

We did not talk more about the holy man the rest of the night. Nor about anything else. We prepared for bed in silence. He did offer me his cot again, but I'd already made my bed on the floor. As he was settling in with a novel, he spoke briefly to ask if I'd mind his keeping the light on for some time yet.

In my long life, it was the first night I'd had to spend at a stranger's. I lay down, my head pillowed on my briefcase, and tried to sleep. But it was difficult. In my sleeplessness, the sombre night seemed to have ripped me from family and job. Had my wife been told I'd have to put up at a schoolteacher's my first night away from home, she wouldn't have believed it. She had always looked upon me as an incorrigible stay-at-home. Her one regret was that I had never once taken her along on a holiday. But holiday travelling for me had always been a depressing affair. I had never before got leave to go to a place of pilgrimage or a hill station.

And this backwater town was neither a place of pilgrimage nor a hill station. Set in the mountains, it could boast only of a veterinary hospital and a Shiva temple where he lived...where he still lives. It is curious how soon we learn to banish to the past the person who walks out of our lives: we refuse to accept that he exists in his own present, outside and independent of our time.

I could not get to sleep till late into the night. The wind lashed at the walls and shook the roof. Whenever a bus passed by on the road below, shadows of trees conjured by its headlights swept along the wall. The hiss of the bus tyres on the wet road resonated along the cliffs and lingered in the air.

Once, as a bus passed, the schoolteacher raised his head off the pillow, squinted at the clock, sighed deeply, and said, "This bus is bound for Bhuvali," and again, when another bus approached blowing its horn, "That's going to Ramnagar." Eyes closed, I pretended to sleep – until the pretense was seized by sleep and dragged into the girth of a dream. When I woke up again, it was after midnight; the lamp had been put out and the room was utterly dark. For a moment, I couldn't place where I was or who was this man sleeping on the cot, turned over on his side.

When I awoke in the morning I found an oblong sun waiting at the bedside. A cool bright day filled the room. The cot was empty. The tea things lay round the stove on the floor. A breeze knocked and thumped outside.

The clock, unbelievably, read ten; I couldn't recall having overslept this long before. I washed hurriedly, put my thermos and a tumbler in the duffel bag, and rifled through the sheaf of papers which included a postcard he – my estranged brother – had written to me a fortnight ago. Then I went out to look for the schoolteacher.

He wasn't there. What hit my eyes instead was a stately mountain. The mountain rose solid and rugged into the air, rooted firmly in the rocky ground, unmoving, real – so unlike the mountains that had cartwheeled yesterday at a distance as the bus sped by. It soared above the town nestling in its shade. The rain and the darkness had concealed it from me before. Now, this instant, I awoke fully to its splendour. I was right here. This was not simply another wayside town but the destination, a world complete in itself, isolated, but not lost, in a dense forest – contrary to what we had imagined back at home – a self-sustaining town, it had a shopping area, a bus station, a hospital, a temple, a high school...

The school stood on flat ground. Yellowish clumps of trees sprinkled the town, which spread out above and below the shopping area. In a tree some way below, I caught a glimpse of the schoolteacher with an axe in this hands...and that cleared up the mystery of the thwacking, thumping sounds that had wakened me. The axe in his hands rose and fell rhythmically on the branches, which dropped down with a swishing rustle.

I set out downhill on the road we had ascended yesterday. Soon the sunlit, grey roof-stones of the shops came into view. Smoke from the cooking fires in the sheds and the market noises floated up.

I went over to sit in the open on a bench in front of one of the eating places buzzing with flies. It was cold despite the sun: the sun had merely cast a web of illusion over a chill reality. I ordered tea.

"Only one tea, Sa'bji?"

I turned to gaze into a pair of bloodshot, drugged eyes fastened on me. He was a holy man, stark naked but for a G-string, lazing on a bench outside the adjacent tea-shop: an Aghori Baba – one who belonged to the Order of the Naked. Quietly I ordered another glassful.

"You came yesterday?" he said, relinquishing his earthly love for the bench he was sitting on.

"You're staying with our schoolteacher?" He came over to sit on my bench.

I could do no more than mumble "yes" to his pronouncements. I thought he had an uncanny gift for reading one's mind. Were he to tell me that I had sired two children and had come from Delhi, I wouldn't have been surprised. But he did not speak another word. His attention was now riveted on the tea in his hands.

"Where are you coming from?" I ventured to ask him later.

He set down his empty glass on the bench and wiped his flowing beard on the crook of his elbow.

"Ask me where I am going to. I am here only for a few days." His red-streaked eyes reflected complete unconcern.

"Where have you set up camp, Baba?"

For a moment I thought his little finger was raised heavenwards; but mercifully it came to rest short of the heavens and pointed to a summit just beginning to emerge from the shimmering morning mist.

"Isn't that where the Shiva temple is?" I could not repress the flutter of excitement and curiosity that the temple aroused in me.

"Don't you call it a Shiva temple! Call it the Mahakal temple." He threw me a glance of derision and reproach. "Haven't you been here before?"

"This is my first visit."

"The first? Are you sure?" He laughed aloud. "How can you be so sure you haven't seen all this before somewhere? No, no! There is no first time."

"I'm seeing you also for the first time."

"Really?" he said, his sly eyes on me. "And that thing over there?" He pointed to a swaying pine tree that climbed straight up from a ditch across the road.

"Why, that's a tree." I was intrigued. "What's there in it?"

"And what's there in me?" He pulled out a *bidi*

from under his skimpy loincloth and lit it on a live coal from a burning log in the mud-daubed stone oven. "What do you see in me?"

Acrid smoke curled lazily upwards from the glowing end of his *bidi*. I ran my eyes all over his naked body. His bones stood out gleaming in the bleached winter sun: a skeleton bound in coarse brown skin which could withstand cold without a shiver or gooseflesh, but provided warmth to what it held together... No, I had never seen this man before; but, seeing him, I was reminded of the bundle of bones and ashes of my father that I'd carried for immersion from Delhi to Kankhal. Had the jostling, rumbling train somehow put the bones together, the reconstructed form could well have resembled the live skeleton before me...and then it struck me that even if one had not seen a certain man before, the latter could still bring back to life another who was once alive and now was no more. What I was seeing in him was not the man who sat so placidly beside me on the bench but a reflection of another, long since dead.

"Are you on a sight-seeing trip?" His watery eyes held on to me.

I kept silent.

He moved over closer to me. "You must have come for a *darshan* of the Baba. Am I right?"

"Well," I stared at him.

"Do you know the way?" He spoke very softly. "He lives on the way to the temple. Go up the rock steps until you come to a track. Turn off along it; it will lead you straight to him."

"Will it be possible to see him now?"

"You can try. It should be no problem unless he has retired to his cell. If he is inside, don't disturb him. He is not keeping well."

"Is he ill?"

There must have been something in my voice which irked him. "Illness is all a part of life. The body is vulnerable."

What he had said gave me no cause to worry. But I was a little surprised that he should not have put even a word about his illness in his message to me. Was he afraid I would have brought our mother along also? I laughed to myself at his fear. How could Mother, who could not climb even the stairs in the house, have stood the rigours of a day-long bus journey to a height of 6800 feet?

I rose to my feet without a word. The Aghori Baba looked up. "What, leaving already!"

"How long will it take to reach there?"

"A lifetime." He smiled. "But if you don't lose your way, you might make it in half an hour."

I filled my thermos with drinking water from the tea-shop. As I took out my wallet to pay for the two glassfuls of tea, the Baba spoke up, "Make it three. I'll have another." I did not even turn around, but paid up and took the road uphill.

The mountainside inclined steeply upwards like an outstretched palm. There were trees all over but none beside the road to give shade. Before long, sweat ran down my body like a mountain stream. My fears of high blood pressure returned, and the loud pounding of my heart rattled my ribs.

The market noises and honking of buses carried up here sleepily. Then even these sounds were lost...and I found myself all alone – not a soul around, no animal, not even air. It struck me that even if I were to keep going up and up, the road would never come to an end – nor would I; I'd forever be struggling up, bathed in sweat, seeing nothing, my mind a blank, my feet refusing to give a damn if I was exhausted.

Up ahead, the road forked into three, like three fingers of an upraised hand. A sign mounted on a tree at the junction, pointing along the right hand path which was the nearest, bore an arrow in white chalk piercing through a four-word legend: *To the Forest Rest-house*. I remembered then about the finger of the Aghori Baba aimed skyward at the Mahakal temple. If the righthand path went off to the rest-house, the middle one could have led only to the temple. I headed up along the middle path.

Long ago there might have been some sort of rock steps here, but now, in this season, the stones fringed with grass blades were slippery with moss. At each step my breath seemed about to snap; still, it wrapped round my trailing foot like a rope to gain me a purchase to pull myself forward. As I hauled myself up, the burden of my years sat heavy on me. But far heavier was my other burden – the legal documents and the messages from the family. I could not help asking myself why it was necessary for me to have to take these papers to him personally: I could as well have left them for the schoolteacher to take care of and gone back by the late evening bus. But then, how would it have looked to have come this far and yet go away without seeing him...go away empty-handed, as it were. After all, he had been living in this part of the world for ten years, and here I was, already despairing on my first day of the visit. He also must have climbed up these same stones a first, fateful time ten years ago – but he had been a young man then. I recalled his face from the latest photograph we had of him – in it he looked what they call "cheerful" in English – reproduced in the newspapers over Father's message (he was alive then): *Please Come Back*... But he not only did not come back, he didn't even write to us. We went from pillar to post in search of him. The police took us on several rounds of the morgues, where we paced the rows of the dead in search of the one who had overnight walked out on us – a stranger.

Trying to recover my breath, I wondered if I would be able to recognise him when I saw him later today.

Sweat dripped into my eyes, weaving a curtain across which a green pine wood on the mountainside glistened. At long last, the temple came into view in a clearing – whitewashed, serene, cool. I sat down on a step, letting the breeze dry me. It was quiet all over: no devotees, no holy men or *sanyasis* who have renounced the world...only a langur which squatted on its haunches on a swinging branch of an ancient tree beside the temple. It regarded me with a momentary curiosity, beating its yard-long tail, before jumping on to the roof. A thud, a rustling of leaves, and nothing else – the silence returned. In the midst of a deep quietude, it seemed the langur and I were the only two who had sought refuge at the shrine of Mahakal, the Timeless One who presides over death. Sometimes the gods do come to our rescue in the form of animals. So had the langur, which had wiped away all my doubts with a swish of its tail. Now when I got up to press forward, I was light of foot.

The temple was not far from here and the ground also had levelled off. A well-trodden path stretched ahead, cleaving the choppy green sea of pine. As the needles fell, a heavy scent diffused into the air. The

Aghori Baba had been right: hardly had I walked another hundred yards or so when I emerged into a clearing – open like a patio, and empty but for grass and rocks. A few steps onwards, a rock to my left caught my eye. I stopped in my tracks as I realised it was no mere rock.

At a second glance it resolved, like a picture puzzle, into a cell built of stones, wood and mud: a fluent union of the natural and the man-made. Its rear portion was flush with a cliff. A rock jutted overhead above three whitewashed stones surmounted by a door before sloping down to the ground on either side.

I walked up the three door-stones. The chain-clasp on the door, unhooked from its staple let into the lintel, hung loosely. It was very quiet inside. I peered through a narrow opening in the door and at first saw nothing but blackness. A pale shaft of daylight entering from an invisible window, or perhaps from the opening in the door itself, penetrated the darkness. A grubby little patch of sun lay on the floor.

Perhaps he lay ill or asleep in his bed somewhere in there. It could be that he had not received my letter and was not expecting me. Or, he might have waited up for me yesterday evening and afterwards assumed that I had put off my visit... I reached out for the chain to rattle it, but it jerked and swung before I could touch it and the door flew open. I made to step back to the lower stone, as if for a shocked moment I wanted to flee, even as he appeared in the doorway. Perhaps more than fear, it was a nervous eagerness to see him better that made me want to fall back, as one does for a better view of a painting on a wall. Be that as it may, he reached out to grip me by my hand and pull me up, and in the scramble my briefcase fell. It clattered down the stones and, with a hiccup, threw out its contents. The property documents, letters, loose sheets – everything flew about and scattered. Mortified, I dropped to the ground to retrieve them. He knelt down beside me, picking up the papers carefully. I stuffed them into the briefcase without so much as an upward glance. Then I felt his hand on my trembling knee.

I turned and saw his hand – not his face yet – for the first time in ten years.

I do not remember how long we sat hunched there. At last, when I raised my head I saw him – his face, his watchful eyes – unmindful of the fact that I had never before seen him with a beard. With his grizzled locks, he resembled a stranger, part half-forgotten brother, part *sanyasi*-recluse.

Yet, in his hand on my knee was a warmth evocative of a distant household and a shared past frozen in memory. The ice began to melt at his touch.

He leaned forward to pick up my briefcase. "Come, let's go in."

I followed him into his cell.

"Please, sit down." His hand on my shoulder, he steered me to one of the two mats on the floor. He himself squatted down opposite me on a rug, his back resting against the wall.

Time dragged by. I was sitting with him in his cell, yet I couldn't bring myself to believe I'd reached the end of my journey.

"Did you get my letter?"

"Yes, I did. But you were supposed to come yesterday."

"I came yesterday, but the bus was late by

three hours."

"Where have you put up?"

"At the schoolteacher's. He took me home."

I longed to ask him then if he had sent the schoolteacher to meet my bus, but I didn't. I was put off by his impassivity and aloofness; he seemed to have drawn a line around himself which I dared not overstep. The thaw that I imagined setting in when he touched me at the doorstep had licked just the outer layers; it had not yet soaked into the core of our being.

"Was it difficult to find your way here?"

"No, not at all. I met an Aghori Baba at a tea-shop. He gave me the necessary directions."

"Did he? What else did he tell you?" He was rather amused.

"Nothing." I looked at him a moment. "Are you ill?"

"He must have told you this. But there is nothing of the sort. It's the old breathing trouble; it gets worse in this weather." It seemed he found talking about his ailment more distressing than living with it.

"Could this high altitude have anything to do with it?"

He shook his head in dissent. "No, I don't think so. You'll recall I suffered from this trouble even when I was at home."

At its mention "home" crept silently in and sat down on its heels between us. He closed his eyes. When a leaf fell out there, it filled the silence in the cell with its patter.

"Is everything over there all right?" he asked drily, his voice keeping its distance from home, yet hovering around it.

"Yes, it's all right."

"The lower floor must be unoccupied, is it?"

"Why should it be?" I didn't follow him. "Mother lives down there."

"Alone, you mean?" He looked hard at me, surprised.

"Yes."

"Doesn't she live with you upstairs?"

"Well, she prefers to live on the lower floor."

He stared at me as if he had no inkling of what had gone on in the house, although I'd written to him about everything I could think of. But he had not seen it happen with his own eyes, and I who had seen it all saw it again from the outside, through his eyes, and began to understand why he was surprised. An outsider might have reason to be surprised to see a woman with a house and three grown sons spend her last days in a corner, alone.

Outside, a branch of a tree creaked and rustled. Suddenly there was a loud thud on the roof, followed by a quick skittering away and unloosening of dust from the ceiling. He went out. I heard his voice carry in the silence. I heard it rise towards the mountain peak and return, until plangent waves caught up with it and bore it gently away.

When he came back I asked him: "Who was there?"

"A langur." He smiled. "They come down from the temple to bask in the sun... Have you been to the temple yet?"

"Not yet. But I hear it's very old."

"Not all that old, perhaps. But the Shiva idol is. It was found buried in the mountainside here. I'll take you to the temple one of these days... Would you like some tea?"

"Who will make it? You?"

"Who else is there?" He laughed. "It'll be ready in no time."

He walked across the cell to a curtain at the rear. He gathered it to one side. It gave on to an underground recess which sloped backwards. There was a low wooden seat in a corner, and beside it stood an earthenware carafe and two clean brass tumblers. In the wall above it was an air vent which could pass for a window: it framed a gnarled branch of a tree, grey rocks, and a slice of the sky suspended in humming silence: nothing moved but the wind. I thought to myself: he lives here alone, day in, day out, in the cold of winter, the rains, the heat of summer. But it was a mere shadow of a thought, without substance, intangible, unconnected to the grim reality. When we see a dead man, we may think either of death, or of the man, or of both, and still fail to register the flesh-and-blood reality of the man meeting his death. But why was I thinking of death? He in whose cell I was sitting was very much alive, although I found it difficult to convince myself that he was the same person I had come to see.

He returned with tea in two tumblers and a dish of salted *shakarparas* on a bronze tray.

"Why don't you move over out of the draft?" he said, setting the tray down on a low slatted board between us.

I took my tumbler and shifted back against the wall. Huddled opposite each other across the narrow cell, we kept to ourselves, while the wind rattled the door now and then and shook the trees.

"The tea smells of burning wood, doesn't it?" he observed.

"Don't you have a kerosene stove?"

"Kerosene is not readily available here. But there's plenty of firewood. I can collect enough during my morning walk. It also helps in keeping the cold away... Come on, take some *shakarparas*. It used to be your favourite dish."

I took some, grateful that he should still remember such a trivial thing, although I'd have suspected he knew little about us, living as he did mostly on the lower floor with Mother. Rarely would he come upstairs. Even my children he met only when they went down to the courtyard to play.

We sipped our tea in silence. He asked no questions about home, which was surprising. But perhaps it was all to the good, for what could he possibly have asked me about, or, at what point could I have picked up the narrative of the ten long years which separated us? It was enough we had a few hours to ourselves. Already noon was wearing off, and shadows had begun to descend from the peaks facing the cell.

A shadow reached out between us, too, delimiting the darker corner where he sat from my side of the room opposite the door, where a thin strip of wan afternoon light sprawled over the threshold in a still moment.

"How are the children?"

"Fine," I said. "Munni has started going to college."

"And the little one?"

"She's grown up now." I grinned as I thought of her. "She wanted to come along."

"Well?"

"She has never been to a mountain. She said she wanted to see where *Tayaji* lived."

"She was very small when...," he trailed off.

When I left home... I was prompted to complete the sentence for him, but I didn't. I let it hang unfinished around the seed of pain at the heart of a deadened grief. But that perhaps is the way grief lasts a lifetime. Buried deep down.

There was no further mention of the children. He picked up the tray with the leftovers and went into the recess behind the curtain.

I sat alone in the dusky light of the cell. Outside, the shadows were thickening on the ground, but the sun still lingered on the humped mountain. A flight of crows winged downwards, shattering the placid atmosphere with their shrill cawing.

He came back in, a hurricane lamp in his hand. As he set it down on the squat board in the middle, he glanced up at me. In that brief moment it seemed he had something important, something crucial on his mind, which he was struggling hard with himself to tell me about. But hesitation got the better of him, and he took his seat quietly.

He sat with his head bowed, the lamplight playing upon his thoughtful profile, the greying hair, the swell of his shoulders, the curve of his neck... It was as if I were seeing my father again in my childhood, the way he would concentrate on the arithmetic sums on my slate, while my fascinated gaze kept wandering off to his neck.

"Does he come to see you?"

"Who?" I started. Was he talking about Father? The next instant I realised he was talking about our elder brother, who had moved out to another part of the city. "Oh yes, he does. Sometimes. In fact, it's he who sent me here."

"What for?"

"He wants us to sell the house. I've brought the sale deed for you to sign." At once I felt relieved. The task for which I had undertaken the long journey was done. How incredibly, wonderfully simple it had turned out to be in the end!

He raised his head. His eyes ran over the briefcase lying on the floor. Slowly then, an understanding dawned on him of what the papers he had helped retrieve from his doorstep were all about.

He looked at me rather wearily. "If you sold the house," he said slowly, "where would Mother live?"

"It's up to her. She can live with either of us."

"And what about you?"

"I'll have to rent a house. In fact, I've already found one."

"So all the decisions have been made. What could I say in the matter now?"

"You too have a share in the property."

"Do I?" He laughed. "I left it all a long time ago."

I looked on at him in silence.

"Is it really necessary to sell the house?"

"Perhaps not. But our brother wants to buy property in Dehradun. He needs cash."

"So he'd sell our father's house?" There was just an edge of sarcasm to his voice.

"How else can he hope to raise the money?"

"But Father pumped all his savings and benefits into it."

"I know. But he's gone."

"True. Still, how can his things cease to be his?"

I gaped at him. Amazing, I thought, and felt like asking how come, having renounced the world, he was still concerned whether the house was sold or retained.

He leaned forward, a smile of reminiscence on his lips. "You know, you were in the final year of the M.A. degree when Father bought the house. We didn't have electricity then, and you'd study by the light of a lantern in your rooftop room."

"Yes, I remember."

"You were married in the courtyard below."

The courtyard, the rooftop room – what was he driving at? Obviously, he wasn't talking about the house itself. What he was saying was something very different, but I failed to grasp it in my irritation.

Out of the corner of my eye I saw what looked like the blazing eyes of some wild animal flash past the air vent in the side wall. It gave me quite a turn. "What was that?"

"Lightning."

My fear was now replaced with worry. "I must leave. It's going to be difficult to go down if it starts raining."

"You needn't hurry."

"The schoolteacher will be worried."

"He knows you are here." Then, after a moment's hesitation, he added, "Why don't you stay with me tonight?"

I'd come prepared with an answer. "It's my blood pressure," I said, trying not to sound foolish. "It may not be good for me to stay overnight at such a height."

I knew I was making a fool of myself, for I was going to spend the night on the mountain anyway. But the thought of spending it with him in his cell was unbearable. I could spend the night with someone either well-known or a total stranger. He was neither; I felt distant and close to him at the same time, which was probably why I had been sent to see him in the first place.

I took my bag and got up to leave.

"Wait a minute. I'll be right back." He went into the back and emerged presently with an umbrella in one hand and a flashlight in the other. "Keep this," he said, giving me the umbrella. "Let me walk you part of the way."

He stepped down the three whitewashed door-stones, reaching out his hand behind him to steady me at the same time. His touch, so gentle, surged into my veins, seeking out the timorous memories crouched out of sight, even as the love and affection of yesteryear returned to light the darkness... Was he the very same person who had left us for good?

Up in front, I saw him stop and turn round. "Well," he said with a laugh, "I thought you were following me."

I hurried my steps. Darkness lay under a thin, glowing veil cast by twinkling stars in a clear, dense sky. And to think, only a short while ago there had been a flash of lightning! Unbelievable!

He walked on effortlessly ahead of me, the beam of his flashlight picking the way, the wayside bushes, trees, rocks. A bird flapped among the leaves and flew away overhead screeching into the darkness. Suddenly, as my lunchbox bumped against the thermos in my shoulder-bag, I realised I didn't have my briefcase with me.

"My briefcase...I've left it behind in your cell."

"Never mind, it will be safe there. You can get it tomorrow."

He stopped and turned towards me. "Is any of your writing in it?" he asked impulsively.

For the first time during the day he had mentioned my writing. I'd assumed that he must have long since forgotten that I ever wrote. Anyway, writing, for me, had been something almost illegitimate, rather like a private disease not to be openly discussed.

"No, there's none. It contains only the property documents and some letters meant for you."

We resumed walking.

"I haven't seen any of your stories in a long time."

"I haven't written much. There is so much to do at the newspaper office... Do you get magazines here?"

"Not regularly. The schoolteacher brings some from time to time from the library... I remember seeing one of your stories in an issue way back."

I kept my pace behind him, my heart pounding away in its slimy shell of shame. Several years ago I'd written a story which unfortunately got into print – indeed, it was written for publication all right. It was not so much about the one who had left home as about those left behind. Both Mother and Father, but Mother more than Father, were hopeful that he would return immediately if he ever came across the story. To say nothing of returning, he hadn't even dropped us a miserable postcard... I was glad he could not see my shame in the dark. But the hurt I had learned over the years to suppress surfaced again. "You," I blurted, "you didn't even write to us!" My voice caught in my throat and I was doubly ashamed. I had resolved before leaving Delhi that I would not say anything of this sort, but now it was out there between us, past us, stumbling on the bright round spot of light on the jungle path.

"It would have been futile," he said.

"You know how we looked for you everywhere?"

No, it was useless to go on. How could he, from his peaceful summit, comprehend the hurry-scurrying torment of the beetles on distant plains? He could not have known what it felt like going on endless rounds of the hospitals, railway platforms, bus stations, or checking the updated police lists of missing persons, or staring into the faces of the dead in the morgues, or placing ads in the newspapers: *Please come back, Mother is ill...*

"I still think it would have been futile."

"You could have at least informed us you were safe."

"Suppose I'd done it, would that have made it easier for you to bear the pain?"

"I'm not talking about pain."

"What are you talking about then?"

I groped in my heart for an answer but found none. I could not lay my finger on anything, neither pain nor Mother's old age, nor my own failures. Everything would still have turned out the way it had. More or less.

"What was the point then in writing home after ten years?"

He was silent a while. "Maybe I shouldn't have." He took a deep breath. "I took all of ten years to write to you. Long enough, I thought, that it should no longer make a difference to you whether I was alive or not."

There was in his tone a rare detachment – otherwise manifest in the trees, the rocks, the streams – above the pain and hurt of embroiled humanity. It had taken him ten austere years of solitude to acquire this detachment.

I heard a rumbling on the slope below us, as if a rock had come loose and was hurtling down.

"What's that noise?"

"It's a cascade. I bring fresh water from there."

"Isn't it rather too far away?"

"Not really. As a matter of fact, the stream flows by just a short way below the cell. I'll show you the place tomorrow."

So he fetched water himself, did he. Instantly, my fatigue, my shame, and the lingering hurt dissolved. The sudden quiet resounded with the purling, splashing water of the hilly stream. The evening prayer bells tinkled in the temple above.

"You should go back," I said. "I can find my way now."

"All right," he agreed. But he made no move to go. I could not tear myself away, either.

"I'll come again tomorrow," I said reassuringly.

"Is it all right at the schoolteacher's? He has only one small room. You can shift into the rest-house, if you like."

"No, that will not be necessary. I'm quite comfortable there. Besides, it's only a matter of another day or two."

Another day or two – the words had tumbled out of my mouth unawares. They swung to and fro, rocked by the wind and the temple bells.

I left hurriedly. I headed down the slope towards the bend in the path. As I reached it, I turned and saw him standing at the spot where I'd left him...silent and unmoving.

The lights were strung out in a festoon along the road below. A mist hung over the sleepy town. Had he also gone to sleep by now or was he awake in his cell? I'd met him after fully ten years and still... Couldn't I have spent even one night with him? You are a writer, I told myself, yet you readily give a wide berth to raw reality when you encounter it, as if living and truth and writing bore no relation to one another; as if each hung like a cold corpse from its own separate gallows. And if I had to run away like this, why did I stay even for a single night here? I ought to have hurried to get his signature on the documents and caught the next bus home. What was the point in staying on in town if we had to spend the night under different roofs? Why did all of us, my brothers and sisters, dry up like wilted stalks at the moment of reckoning? How was it that at a certain point all our love doused itself in sand and ashes? How could we leave one another to his or her fate and stand aloof? Wasn't it the tyranny of this sinful indifference which had driven him from home?

Even as I plunged downhill, I sank deeper into the mire of guilt and self-recrimination. With every step toward the schoolteacher's, I burned the more intensely with a desire to become invisible or else somehow vanish in his cot for the night and leave for Delhi first thing next morning.

The schoolteacher was busy in the kitchen, and I got in unnoticed. I could not summon enough courage to face him right then. All I wanted was to change into my night clothes and burrow into the cot. A brazier glowed in the room. As I approached it, I felt suddenly very exhausted and cold and feverish. In the core of my being, my feverish heart and shivery body tortured and played with each other, while "I" stood to one side. This was good in itself, providing as it did some measure of relief to a layman unable to renounce the world like the *sadhus* and *sanyasis*, but who can nevertheless, if only briefly, walk out of his body and heart and their tensions and, disembodied, stand apart. But I was not long in luck. Hardly had I stretched out on the cot when I started at a sound from the direction of the kitchen. I turned to see the schoolteacher standing in the doorway, staring hard at me as if he had caught me red-handed.

"When did you come in?" he asked.

"Just a little while ago. I'm not feeling well," I offered by way of excuse.

It mollified him somewhat and he came over. "I told you last night to sleep on the cot. In the rains, the floor gets rather damp and chilly."

He placed his palm on my forehead and felt my pulse at the wrist. "No fever," he concluded. "But you must be exhausted. I have some brandy. I'd advise you to have a sip. It will warm you up."

He took out a bottle from the cupboard and brought two glasses. I sat up on the cot. Opposite the two of us sat the glowing brazier like some mysterious hill deity whom we had got together to appease. As we indulged ourselves, a bird out in the darkness pecked insistently into the silence and scattered it with strange, entreating cries.

"It's the *ninira* bird. Its call puts the children to sleep." He took a swallow from his glass. "Would you like to have a drop of warm water in your drink?"

"No, don't bother. This is okay... Do you have liquor shops in town?"

"No. I get my occasional bottle from Almora or Bhuvali, thanks to an obliging bus driver."

Thanks to the brandy and the brazier, my limbs began to unloosen and the knots melt away. Although the feelings of guilt and disquiet did not vanish altogether, they withdrew a pleasant distance to hover with my soul. I grew light-headed, dimly aware that the schoolteacher was regarding me with a quizzical expression.

"Have you been to see Babaji?"

I stared at his yellow teeth. Perhaps he did not suspect that the one whom he called Baba could in some way be related to me. People hardly ever give it a thought that the holy men too come from ordinary homes and have ordinary pasts.

"Was he in his cell?"

"Where else could he have been?"

"Anywhere. Until some time ago, he used to roam all over. He would even come down for shopping."

"Doesn't he go out any more?"

"I don't know. I haven't seen him around lately, though. There was a time I'd go to see him in his cell and help him with the chores. But I found his behaviour rather strange and discouraging, and stopped going there."

"What did you find so strange?"

He gazed into his palm, as if the answer were written there. Then he took a sip from his glass. "Last summer I used to fetch water for him," he said, looking up at me. "But he did not like it. One morning I was returning from the waterfall when he met me on the way. Could I gather some firewood for him, he asked. 'Why not?' I said. Thereupon, he asked with a smile if I could cook his meals also. 'No problem,' I said at once. After all, he used to eat only once a day. 'And I – what would I do?' he said. 'Why, Baba,' I said, 'you must spend your time in meditation and prayers, for which you renounced the world.' Do you know what he said then?"

The schoolteacher fell silent, staring into the sibilant flames in the brazier.

"What did he say?" I demanded.

"He said, 'How can you meditate upon One you know nothing about?'"

"Did he?"

"I said if it was so, why did he leave his family to come here. Can you imagine what he said? He said, 'I have left nothing; I only came away.' There was nothing I could do then but to leave the pail on the spot and walk away. I wonder how can a man who does not like being served can serve Him."

The schoolteacher sighed, and resumed after a while, "I also live here alone, but I have a job to do. Why is he here? He does not read his scriptures, nor say his prayers, nor meditate, nor hold discourses. He does not even have a word of counsel for the visitors who call on him to pay their obeisance."

"Still, people go to see him?"

"They do. Remember, you too came from far off just to see him!"

"I'd heard about his fame," I said lamely.

"So do others. Some come to get their wish or to get his blessing, others are merely curious."

I felt the schoolteacher's penetrating glance. I looked into myself and found neither desire nor curiosity – nothing but a gossamer connecting thread that neither the schoolteacher could grasp nor I pull down.

"Shall I lay the meal? It's late."

He went into the kitchen. I kept sitting on the bed. Outside, crickets chirped monotonously. The brandy had kindled in me a gentle, cosy fire; slowly its warmth spread to combat the frost in my marrow and the cumulative exhaustion of a lifetime.

"Have you dozed off?"

I came to with a start; the warmth had indeed lulled me to sleep. He set down two trays of food on the floor: *dal*, a vegetable, thick hot *chapattis*... He had prepared the meal himself. I envied him his simplicity in extending hospitality to me without demanding to know who I was. I was so touched I wanted to confess that his unorthodox Baba was none other than my own brother, but I got over the impulse immediately; it would have only embarrassed him... Some facts are wholly unnecessary and had better be left alone.

"You'll stay here for a few days, won't you?" His manner was easy, friendly and eager.

"No, I must push off tomorrow," I said somewhat self-consciously. "I could get only two days' leave."

"Where do you work?" This was the first direct question he had put to me about myself, and he sounded so genuinely concerned that I was grateful to him. I told him about my newspaper work, about my children, my household. He listened quietly. When I'd finished and still he didn't speak up, I began to have doubts if he had heard me at all. I looked up into his face. In the pale moonlight from the window, I saw his wide open eyes fastened on me. It unnerved me. Whatever was going on in his head?

"Look, why don't you stay on for another couple of days? You've come so far from home, it would be a shame if you had to go back so soon."

"What's the point? What shall I do here?"

"You can be with Baba that much longer. He is all alone these days."

"Why don't you call on him more often yourself?"

"Well, I wouldn't know what to talk to him about."

"Anyway, he left home on his own. And to live alone is not such a great misfortune, either. After all, you also live alone," I reasoned with him.

"It's different with me. I go away to Almora for a few days every month. If I could find a better house here, I'd even bring my family over." As another thought occurred to him, a look of puzzlement came into his eyes. "I can't understand something," he said ambiguously. "Many years have passed since Baba came to live here. But, so far, no one from his family seems to have ever visited him."

I had a lingering suspicion that he had all along known everything about me, but had taken care not to show it in his face.

"Probably his family doesn't know he's here."

"You mean in all these years they couldn't even find out his whereabouts?"

"They must have tried their best. But it's such a vast country. How can one comb every part of it?"

He stared into the darkness outside, lost in thought. At last, he said, "Perhaps he never had much of a family. There are some who leave their homes in search of God out of sheer loneliness."

"You should have asked him."

"He tells about himself as little as about God. Sometimes I doubt if he is a true *sanyasi*; I doubt if he has truly renounced the world and taken to God."

What was he if not a *sanyasi*, I asked myself. Ten years ago he had left everyone at home crying; now could he leave God as well? The night held out no answer.

I lay down on my bedding on the floor while the schoolteacher stretched out on his cot, like the previous night.

But unlike last night, the room was not completely dark; the moon hung low in the kitchen window, shedding a pale luminous dust on the things in the room. I lay awake for a long time. When my thoughts turned to my family, they seemed to belong to another world; and when I thought of my brother living the life of a hermit, his seemed to be yet another world unknown to us. These different little worlds abutted one another, yet they were millions of miles apart. How did each come to its isolation? The question was painful and frightening. I tucked it under me for the night, turning over on my side.

Crows wheeled overhead, scores and scores of them. Cawing shrilly, they descended to settle on the rocks, pathways, branches, treetops, everywhere. Their sharp cries cracked the sky.

The schoolteacher and I had gone to the bus stand. In the adjoining shed, there was a small crowd of passengers. Stray dogs and coolies dozed outside the eating places across the road. The schoolteacher made his way to the ticket window. It was closed. He rapped on it with his knuckles several times before a head peered out. Soon he returned with the information that there was no advance booking. "You'll get your ticket on the bus itself," he told me.

"Did you ask what time it leaves?"

"There is only one direct bus to Delhi, in the evening at six. Another leaves at eight, but then you'd have to catch a connecting bus at Bhuvali."

A lot of time to go till six o'clock, I told myself. I had already packed my things. In fact, I had left my trunk at a sweet-shop nearby to save a detour to the schoolteacher's on the way back from the summit in the afternoon. I carried with me only my hold-all and the umbrella my brother had given to me the night before.

"Come, let's have another tea. You've a long climb ahead of you."

We had had our tea before starting out for the bus stand. But it was so cold out here that I couldn't resist the temptation of another by the warm oven at the tea-shop.

The schoolteacher had been unusually quiet since the morning, when he had asked me again not to be in a hurry to leave for Delhi. However, he did not insist when I told him that I had to get back to write my column for the newspaper the next day. We did not talk about the Baba any more. We seemed to have reached a tacit agreement to black him out of our conversation, even as the clouds had blacked out his cell, the temple, the forest rest-house, and everything else up there. The sky was overcast, but it did not look as if it would rain; it promised to be one of those days when there is neither rain nor sunshine. A grey mass of spent clouds had piled up, trapped between the valley below and the peaks above.

"These clouds pass over Bhuvali to reach here," the schoolteacher remarked. "The main rainclouds are borne to Ranikhet and Nainital, while the dregs are banished to this penal colony...to serve their sentence, as it were."

"Well!" I took another sip of tea. "Don't these clouds move on somewhere?"

"They go nowhere. Only the crows do. Look at the swarms of them!" he said laughingly.

Indeed, the crows were all over – over the peak, the housetops, the trees...

"Aren't they a sight for a small town like this? They say this place carries a curse that all its dead will be reborn as crows."

"Still, people live here."

"Yes, they do, because they also believe that these crows in turn attain salvation on dying," he explained soberly. "This town is a sort of transit camp for men – and crows – on their way to deliverance."

The schoolteacher was no longer smiling. A pensive look in his eyes, he gazed quietly at the black legions of crows and the little town lost in misty clouds. A penal colony, he had called it, for the clouds from Bhuvali, the furthest end of the earth: a province for the spirits of the dead and the crows. He had spent half his life here.

He wouldn't let me pay for the tea.

"Try to get back early. I'll see you here." He hesitated a moment before adding, "And pay him my respects also."

"Why don't you come along? He'd be glad to see you." I'd rather not have had to go to him alone this time.

He was caught unawares. "No, no," he said evasively. "I can always see him later. But for you this may well be the last opportunity."

With that, he turned away abruptly and disappeared into the shopping quarter.

The road uphill was muddy, and a light drizzle had begun. It was midday, yet a darkness was creeping up. I unfurled the umbrella over my head and continued to walk up with long strides. By the time I reached the rock steps which led to the temple, I was panting. I felt like sitting down to recover my breath; it would not do to rush in on him gasping and sweating and out of sorts. On the other hand, the sooner I was on my way again, the longer I could be with him before I had to get back in time for the six o'clock bus. I was up and off in a couple of minutes.

Off the path down on the slope was a beautiful little cottage which must have been nestling there since the times of the English...a relic from the old, familiar world: lighted fireplaces, carefree laughter of girls in the passages, music on the radio. It called for a deliberate effort to think that up here in the outlands there lived ordinary, happy people who had nothing to do with the secluded cell of my brother, the naked ascetic, or the loneliness of the schoolteacher. Within similar four snug walls I'd spent the forty years of my life. But from these misty heights the familiar and the known seemed suddenly to fade into unreality... And then, without forewarning, a fear gripped me: What would happen to me if, in a convulsive moment, my world were to turn inside out? I'd probably beat the darkness in vain with my inadequate wings like an insect nipped from the living room between thumb and forefinger and thrown out the window at night, unable ever after to find its way back in. But, mercifully, the moment passed and I could laugh at myself. I reached into my coat pocket and touched my bank passbook; I touched the muffler round my neck, given to me by my wife on our last anniversary; my patent leather wallet carried photographs of both my children; I was part-owner of a house in Delhi; and there were books with my name on their covers – all solid, incontrovertible proof of my earthly existence. I was born forty years ago, quickened by the essence of life everlasting. It seemed impossible that it should now betray me and let me be turned into a mere moth. No, there was no cause for fear. Reassured, I hastened towards the cell of my brother, glad that in a few hours a bus would take me back to the world where I belonged.

I sighed with relief when the cell came into view. I almost ran up the three door-stones. Dull lamplight shone through a fissure in the door. As I made to rattle the chain, I heard voices inside. Was there someone in there with him? I heard his voice, and it sounded as if he were praying or talking to himself, or mumbling in sleep or in a stupor of high fever. I looked in through the fissure and caught sight of him standing below the air vent.

Even today I haven't been able to get over the scene – though perhaps scene may not be the word for it. The person I saw through the fissure was neither a hermit (heretic or otherwise) nor the brother I'd known. Completely oblivious of his surroundings, he was talking to himself and laughing at the same time. Awe-struck, I stood helplessly at the door, torn between fear and old ties of love, even as another part of me pushed headlong in to cling to him, screaming at him in bewilderment as to what he thought he was doing, whoever was he talking to, whatever was he laughing at.

They say when the soul is rendered dumb the body speaks: the blood rumbles in the dead silence and we hear our heart beat. I do not remember when my hand, of its own volition, rattled the chain or when he opened the door, but I do remember the touch of his palm upon my shoulder and the sound of his words in my ears: "What held you up? I've been waiting for you since morning."

His voice was so matter-of-fact, calm and collected that my head jerked upwards. I was astonished to see him smiling serenely. Was he the same person who only a minute before was laughing to himself and raving like a madman?

"You..." I started to ask him but changed my mind at the last moment and left the question uncomposed. A door inside me swung closed. In the past, too, I'd closed so many doors behind me that one more made no difference.

"Your hand feels very warm," I said instead. "Are you all right?"

Gently, he removed his hand from my shoulder and said, as though he had not heard me, "Come in. It's very cold outside."

I stood his umbrella in a corner and took off my shoes. It was as cold in here as outside. The solitary lamp cast a cold yellow smudge of light in the bare room.

"Where have you been so long?" he said.

"I went to the bus stand to reserve a seat on the evening bus."

He said nothing. In the wan circle of light his pale face, his greying beard, his thick black eyebrows – nothing registered any flicker of emotion. The gaze he directed on me was impassive, neither intimate nor stand-offish.

"On my morning walk, I passed by the rest-house. I happen to know the overseer in charge of it. He can spare a room for you."

"What's the use?"

"You can take a few days off. You need not be in a hurry to go back."

His voice carried just a hint of insistence and a faint trace of a distant affection. His apparent self-control made the mild concern all the more difficult and painful to bear.

"Would it make you happy if I stayed?"

He gave a little laugh. "Would you be staying for my sake alone?"

"Who else is here? I came only to see you."

"I thought, maybe, you'd like to spend some days here."

"Do you want me to?"

"What I want is irrelevant." He fell silent. Then he added slowly, "Why don't you give yourself some holiday?"

"Back home, they'd think I too had gone your way. Isn't one *sanyasi* in the family already more than a handful?"

"Do they really think I'm a *sanyasi*?" He smiled. "I live here the same as I did over there. There's only been a change of place."

"Is that all? You think nothing else has changed? That you haven't changed either?"

"Have I? What do you think?" I thought I detected a glint of amusement in his eyes.

"I never imagined I'd ever see you again in this life."

"In this life? What do you mean?" He looked at me in amazement. "Is there any life other than this one?"

I gave him a cautious, searching glance. Was he playing with me? But his gaze was unwavering and steady, and there was sadness in his voice.

"If we live but once and if living here is no different from what it was back home, what was the point then in...in your change of address?"

"There is a point," he said slowly. "Over there, I did not matter to anyone."

"And here?"

"Here there is no one to whom I should care if I mattered."

"How is it possible to ... to give up your own people?"

He was lost in thought. Dull daylight seeped into the small room. He let his head drop to his chest until only the thatch of his grey hair showed. The face that I'd seen creased into laughter only a short time ago was now a flat shadow in a dark pool.

"No," he spoke at last. "It's not possible. That is why I wrote to you. It is not enough just to give up certain people or things and hope to become a *sanyasi*..."

He had leaned farther away from the wall. His eyes were closed. The door moved as a wind rose and swept leaves and dust inside.

Suddenly, he opened his eyes.

"Who is there?" He looked startled.

"No one," I said. But in a moment I heard footsteps outside and saw a group of three or four come up to the door-stones.

"Just have a look. See who they are," he said to me.

I went over and opened the door wide. Some three or four gentlemen stood out there. They were accompanied by two women. When they saw me, one of the men stepped forward to inquire if the Baba was in.

Even before I could answer him, I heard my brother's voice behind me: "Please be seated under the tree. I'll be with you in a moment."

At his voice, they folded their hands in humility. I

moved over to let my brother pass. As he went down
to the bottom step, the visitors took turns to come
forward to touch his feet. The last one was the
younger of the two women. She was very young and
was draped in a black shawl. She looked up to the
Baba, sank to her knees and bowed until her head
touched his feet. She remained in this position for
what seemed a long time.

And throughout, my brother stood still. He spoke
not a word, nor did he once hold out his hand
in blessing.

Finally, he turned to me. "Wait inside," he said. "It
shouldn't take very long." He looked rather ill at ease.
Wearily, I watched him. Was he ashamed of me
before the visitors?

I went back in and turned down the lamp so that the
grey daylight could advance further into the cell. The
group of callers was sitting with him on a low
whitewashed platform beneath an old plane tree
which stood over to one side. Fragments of their
voices as they talked to the Baba carried in, but I
heard him say nothing in reply. I recalled, with a
feeling of shame, the question I'd put to him about
leaving the family. He had left us, but would these
strangers leave him alone? What did he have to offer
them? Why did they keep coming to him? Most
certainly they got from him something about which I
knew nothing. Was I looking at a stranger in the guise
of my brother, asking him questions that had no
relevance in this place?

And then my mind floated back across several years
to the time I'd done the rounds of the morgues in
search of him. It seemed to me I was one of the many
lining up in front of the platform to receive his

blessing...to catch a glimpse of him from close up. But it was another time, another place: instead of the platform there were slabs of ice on which corpses lay like dead fish. As I lingered by the slabs looking for him, the attendant in the morgue pushed me from behind. "Hurry up," he said rudely, "there are others, too, who have to identify their dead. Move on, will you?" Their dead...the other people...I was jostled and pushed and carried onwards, on and on, up through the next ten years. I imagined I was lying on a cold slab of a floor and he was leaning over me, concerned.

"*Chhote!*" he was calling out to me.

I heard him faintly and saw the lantern he held over me. Ten years earlier he had called me by that pet name: *Chhote*, Little Brother. I sat up, startled. Where am I? Was I back home? I stared wide-eyed at him.

"You'd fallen asleep," he said gently. I saw him more clearly now, and saw his blanket around me, warm with the heat of my body.

"Have those people left?"

"They left long ago."

"This blanket? I don't remember..."

"When I came in I saw you shivering, as if you were lying on ice," he said, smiling.

On ice, was it? I emerged from a ten-year-old dream. A faded yellow light reached out across the floor. The sun had come out of the clouds, ready to go down below the horizon. The peaks glittered in the late afternoon light.

He spoke again, very softly, leaning over me: "Do keep lying down, rest some more. I'll make you some tea."

I saw him, a slight smile across his mouth, as if he

too had just got up from another slab of ice, his own, and come out into the light where his present blended with my past. In the lingering moment, it struck me that my gaze and his silence were a kind of preparation – for this moment had instantly spanned the vast speechless desert that stretched away into the past – a preparation for both of us. Perhaps it was for this reason alone that he had called me. He had wanted to break with us, with all of us, one last time. Finally. A clean break.

I rose slowly, folded his blanket and put it away in a corner. I crossed over to the door, put on my shoes and picked up my bag. I looked round at him. He stood there, with the lantern still in his hand, although here in the doorway it was unnecessary.

"I must push off," I said. "It's nearly time for the bus."

He looked on at me in silence. Then he said slowly, "Wait a minute. I'll be right back."

He went into the rear of the cell and returned with my briefcase in his hand in place of the lantern.

"Aren't you overlooking this again?" he said smilingly, giving the briefcase back to me. "I've taken the letters and..." After a momentary pause, he added, "You can see I've signed all the papers."

I saw him turn slightly away. The sun straining through the branches of the plane tree beside his cell fell across his feet. I bent down at his feet to pay my respects, and felt his hand on my head, his fingers stroking my hair, his burning touch sending waves of heat through my body.

I raised my head. The cell looked empty. A black branch of the old tree hanging heavily over the air vent cast a long shadow inside. A spot of the sun had quietly crept up close to his feet... I'd reached the end of my journey.

I picked up my briefcase and came out.

That's about all; there's really nothing left to say. Later, of course, I climbed down the path clinging to the wooded mountainside, awash with the glow of a setting sun. And it led all the way down to Delhi and my friends, the newspaper office, the blazing summer afternoons and my make-believe stories. The school-teacher and the Aghori Baba saw me off at the bus stand. With the passage of time, the misty heights where I met my brother for the last time, and the schoolteacher, and the Aghori Baba have receded in my memory, although sometimes, in unexpected moments, everything returns poignantly in my trou-bled thoughts... The schoolteacher, who stood close up by the bus window, asked me ingenuously if the desire that had made me undertake the journey had been fulfilled. But before I could think what answer to make, the bus pulled out. He ran alongside for a short distance and then fell behind. When I looked round at the Aghori Baba, I saw he had not moved; he had found something more engrossing in the sky overhead – he stood rooted to his spot, looking up at the crows fluttering away over the treetops, wheeling in the air above the pine forest and the temple of the Timeless One, gathering into a clamorous darkness in a darkening sky.

About the translators: KULDIP SINGH has translated some thirty short stories and a documentary novel,
An Island of Salt, working from both Hindi and
Punjabi into English. His translations and his original
English-language poems have been widely published
in India. He also works as a Reader in Physiology at
the Gandhi Medical College in Bhopal, and deputy
director of medical education in the state government
service there.

JAI RATAN has previously worked with Kuldip
Singh in translating Nirmal Verma's stories for the
Readers International volume, *The World Elsewhere.*

DATE DUE